You feel the lines of force, living in Washington, D.C.; feel the struggle for power among the shadowy manifolds surrounding the official government space; read of the unsolved murders, of shadowy people whose jobs are not made clear . . . As a blind person one feels apart from that nebulous world of intrigue and hidden force, on the edge by reason of disability. ("No one harms a blind man.") Now I knew I was part of it, pulled in, on my own. It was frightening.

But they didn't know how much I knew. Snuffle of an approaching boxer, counterpunch right in the face. I have to be bold just to cross the street!

THE BLIND
GEOMETER

The Tor SF Doubles

*forthcoming

KIM STANLEY ROBINSON
THE BLIND GEOMETER

A TOM DOHERTY ASSOCIATES BOOK
NEW YORK

THE BLIND GEOMETER

A TOR Book
Published by Tom Doherty Associates, Inc.
49 West 24 Street
New York, NY 10010

Cover art by Peter Gudynas

ISBN: 0-812-50010-5   Can. ISBN: 0-812-50114-4

Library of Congress Catalog Card Number:

First edition: October 1989

Printed in the United States of America

0 9 8 7 6 5 4 3 2 1

THE BLIND GEOMETER

A. When you are born blind, your development is different from that of sighted infants. (I was born blind, I know.) The reasons for this are fairly obvious. Much normal early infant development, both physical and mental, is linked to vision, which coordinates all sense and action. Without vision reality is ... (it's hard to describe) a sort of void, in which transitory things come to existence when grasped and mouthed and heard—then when the things fall silent or are dropped, they melt away, they *cease to exist.* (I wonder if I have not kept a bit of that feeling with me always.) It can be shown that this sense of object permanence must be learned by sighted infants as well—move a toy behind a screen and very young babies will assume the toy has ceased to exist—but vision (seeing part of a toy [or a person] behind the screen, etc.) makes their construction of a sense of object permanence fairly rapid and easy. With the blind child it is a much harder task, it takes months, sometimes years. And with no sense of an object world, there can be no complementary concept of self; without this concept, all phenomena can be experienced as part of an extended "body." (Haptic space [or tactile space, the space of the body] expanding to fill visual space . . .) Every blind infant is in danger of autism.

"But we also have, and know that we have, the capacity of complete freedom to transform, in thought and phantasy, our human historical existence. . . ."

— Edmund Husserl, *The Origin of Geometry*

C. *Mark point A. Then mark point B. Only one line, AB, can be drawn through these two points.* Say that events, happening hadon by hadon in the unimaginably brief slice of reality that is the present, are points. Connecting these points would then create lines, and the lines figures—figures that would give a shape to our lives, our world. If the world were a Euclidean space, this would make the shapes of our lives comprehensible to us. But the world is not a Euclidean space. And so all our understanding is no more than a reductive mathematics for the world. Language as a kind of geometry.

AB. My first memories are of the Christmas morning when I was some three and a half years old, when one of my gifts was a bag of marbles. I was fascinated by the way the handfuls of marbles felt in my fingers: heavy glass spheres, all so smooth and clickety, all so much the same. I was equally impressed by the leather bag that had contained them. It was so pliable, had such a baggy shape, could be drawn up by such a leathery draw string. (I must tell you, from the viewpoint of tactual aesthetics, there is nothing quite so beautiful as well-oiled leather. My favorite toy was my father's boot.) Anyway, I was rolling on my belly over the marbles spread on the floor (more contact) when I came against the Christmas tree, all prickly and piney. Reaching up to break off some needles to rub between my fingers, I touched an ornament that felt to me, in my excitement, like a lost marble. I yanked on it (and on the branch, no doubt) and—down came the tree.

The alarum afterward is only a blur in my memory, as if it all were on tape, and parts of it forever fast-forwarded to squeaks and trills. Little unspliced snippets of tape: my memory. (My story.)

BA. How often have I searched for snippets before that one, from the long years of my coming to consciousness? How did I first discover the world beyond my body, beyond my searching hands? It was one of my greatest intellectual feats—perhaps the greatest—and yet it is lost to me.

So I read, and learned how other blind infants accomplished the task. I understood better how important my mother had to have been in this process, I began to understand why I felt about her the way I did, why I missed her so.

My own life, known to me through words—the world become a text—this happens to me all the time. It is what T.D. Cutsforth called entering the world of "verbal unreality," and it is part of the fate of the curious blind person.

0. I never did like Jeremy Blasingame. He had been a colleague for a few years, and his office was six doors down from mine. It seemed to me that he was one of those people who are fundamentally uncomfortable around the blind; and it's always the blind person's job to put these people at their ease, which gets to be a pain in the ass. (In fact, I usually ignore the problem.) Jeremy always watched me closely (you can tell this by voice), and it was clear that he found it hard to believe that I was one of the co-editors of *Topological Geometry*, a journal he submitted to occasionally. But he was a good mathematician, and a fair topologist, and we had published some of his submissions, so that he and I remained superficially friendly.

Still, he was always probing, always picking my brains. At this time I was working hard on the geometry of *n*-dimensional manifolds, and some of the latest results from CERN and SLAC and the big new accelerator on Oahu were fitting into the work in an interesting way: it appeared that certain sub-atomic particles were moving as if in a multi-dimensional manifold, and I had Sullivan and Wu and some of the other physicists from these places asking questions about my work in multi-dimensional geometries. With them I was happy to talk, but with Jeremy I couldn't see the point. Certain speculations I once made in conversation with him later showed up in one of his papers; and it just seemed to me that he was looking for help without actually saying so.

And there was the matter of his image. In the sun I perceived him as a shifting, flecked brightness. It's unusual I can see people at all, and as I couldn't really account for this (was it vision, or something else?) it made me uncomfortable.

But no doubt in retrospect I have somewhat exaggerated this uneasiness.

AC. The first event of my life that I recall that has any emotion attached to it (the earlier ones being mere snips of tape that could have come from anyone's life, given how much feeling is associated with them) comes from my eighth year, and has to do, emblematically enough, with math. I was adding columns with my Braille punch, and excited at my new power, I took the bumpy sheet of figures to show my father. He puzzled over it for a while. "Hmm," he said. "Here, you have to make very sure that the columns are in straight vertical rows." His long fingers guided mine down a column. "Twenty-two is off to the left, feel that? You have to keep them all straight."

Impatiently I pulled my hand away, and the flood of frustration began its tidal wash through me (most familiar of sensations, felt scores of times a day); my voice tightened to a high whine: "But *why?* It doesn't *matter*—"

"Yes it does." My father wasn't one for unnecessary neatness, as I already knew well from tripping over his misplaced briefcase, ice skates, shoes. . . . "Let's see." He had my fingers again. "You know how numbers work. Here's twenty two. Now what that means, is two twos, and two tens. This two marks the twenty, this two marks the two, even though they're both just two characters, right? Well, when you're adding, the column to the far right is the column of ones. Next over is the column of tens, and next over is the column of hundreds. Here you've got three hundreds, right? Now if you have the twenty-two over to the left too far, you'll add the twenty in the hundreds column, as if the number were two hundred twenty rather than twenty-two. And that'll be wrong. So you have to keep the columns really straight—"

Understanding, ringing me as if I were a big old church bell, and it the clapper. It's the first time I remember feeling that sensation that has remained one of the enduring joys of my life: *to understand*.

And understanding mathematical concepts quickly led to power (and how I craved that!), power not only in the abstract world of math, but in the real world of father and school. I remember jumping up and down, my dad laughing cheerily, me dashing to my room to stamp out columns as straight as the ruler's edge, to add column after column of figures.

A. Oh yes: Carlos Oleg Nevsky, here. Mother Mexican, father Russian (military advisor). Born in Mexico City in 2018, three months premature, after my mother suffered a bout of German measles during the pregnancy. Result: almost total blindness (I can tell dark from [bright] light.) Lived in Mexico City until father was transferred to Soviet embassy in Washington, D.C., when I was five. Lived in Washington almost continuously since then. My parents divorced when I was ten, and my mother returned to Mexico City when I was thirteen. I never understood that; their whole relationship took place out of earshot, it seemed. But from then on I was wary.

Mathematics professor at George Washington University since 2043.

OA. One cold spring afternoon I encountered Jeremy Blasingame in the faculty lounge as I went to get a coffee refill—in the lounge, where nobody ever hangs out. "Hello, Carlos, how's it going?"

"Fine," I said, reaching about the table for the sugar. "And you?"

"Pretty good. I've got a kind of an interesting problem over at my consulting job, though. It's giving me fits."

Jeremy worked for the Pentagon in military intelligence or something, but he seldom talked about what he did there, and I certainly never asked. "Oh yes?" I said as I found the sugar and spooned some in.

"Yes. They've got a coding problem that I bet would interest you."

"I'm not much for cryptography." Spy games—the math involved is really very limited. Sweet smell of sugar, dissolving in the lounge's bad coffee.

"Yes, I know," Jeremy said. "But—" An edge of frustration in his voice; it's hard to tell when I'm paying attention, I know. (A form of control.) "But this may be a geometer's code. We have a subject, you see, drawing diagrams."

A *subject*. "Hmph," I said. Some poor spy scribbling away in a cell somewhere . . .

"So—I've got one of the drawings here. It reminds me of the theorem in your last article. Some projection, perhaps."

"Yes?" Now what spy would draw something like that?

"Yeah, and it seems to have something to do

with her speech, too. Her verbal sequencing is all dislocated—words in strange order, sometimes."

"Yes? What happened to her?"

"Well . . . Here, check out the drawing."

I put out a hand. "I'll take a look."

"And next time you want coffee, come ask me. I do a proper job of it in my office."

"All right."

AB. I suppose I have wondered all my life what it would be like to see. And all my work, no doubt, is an effort to envision things in the inward theater. "I see it *feelingly*." In language, in music, most of all in the laws of geometry, I find the best ways I can to see: by analogy to touch, and to sound, and to abstractions. Understand: to know the geometries fully is to comprehend exactly the physical world that light reveals; in a way one is then perceiving something like the Platonic ideal forms underlying the visible phenomena of the world. Sometimes the great ringing of comprehension fills me so entirely that I feel I *must* be seeing; what more could it be? I believe that I see.

Then comes the problem of crossing the street, of finding my misplaced keys. Geometry is little help; it's back to the hands and ears as eyes, at that point. And then I know that I do not see at all.

* * *

BC. Let me put it another way. Projective geometry began in the Renaissance, as an aid to painters newly interested in perspective, in the problems of representing the three-dimensional world on a canvas; it quickly became a mathematics of great power and elegance. The basic procedure can be illustrated quickly.

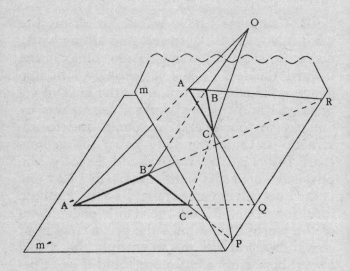

Figure 1

Here a geometrical figure is *projected* from one plane to another (as light, they tell me, projects a slide's image onto a wall). Note that while certain properties of triangle ABC are changed in triangle A'B'C' (lengths of sides, measures of angles), other properties are not: points are still points, lines lines, and certain proportions still hold, among other things.

Now imagine that the visual world is triangle ABC (reduction . . .). But then imagine that it has been projected inward onto something different, not onto a plane, but onto a Moebius strip or a Klein bottle say, or really, onto a manifold much more complex and strange than those (you'd be surprised.) Certain features of ABC are gone for good (color, for instance), but other essential features remain. And projective geometry is the art of finding what features or qualities survive the transformations of projection. . . .

Do you understand me?

A way into the world, a mode of consciousness, a philosophy, a type of being. A vision. A geometry for the self. Non-Euclidean, of course; in fact, strictly Nevskyan, as it has to be to help me, as I make my projections from visual space to auditive space, to haptic space, to the world inside.

OA. The next time I met Blasingame he was anxious to hear what I thought of his diagram. (There could be an acoustics of emotion, thus a mathematics of emotion; meanwhile the ears of the blind do these calculations every day.)

"One drawing isn't much to go on, Jeremy. I mean, you're right, it looks like a simple projective drawing, but with some odd lines crossing it. Who knows what they mean? The whole thing might be something scribbled by a kid."

"She's not that young. Want to see more?"

"Well . . ." This woman he kept mentioning, some sort of Mata Hari prisoner in the Pentagon, drawing geometrical figures and refusing to speak except in riddles . . . naturally I was intrigued.

"Here, take these anyway. There seems to be a sort of progression."

"It would help if I could talk to this *subject* who's doing all these."

"Actually, I don't think so. But"—(seeing my irritation)—"I can bring her by, I think, if these interest you."

"I'll check them out."

"Good, good." Peculiar edge of excitement in his voice, tension, triumph, fear, the anticipation of . . . something. Frowning, I took the papers from him.

That afternoon I shuffled them into my special xerox machine, and the stiff reproductions rolled out of it heavily ridged. I ran my hands over the raised lines and letters slowly.

Here I must confess to you that most geometrical drawings are almost useless to me. If you consider it you will quickly see why: most drawings are two-dimensional representations of what a three-dimensional construction *looks* like. This does me no good, and in fact is extremely confusing. Say I feel a trapezoid on the page; is that meant to be a trapezoid, or is it rather a representation of a rectangle not coterminous with the page it lies on? Or the conventional representation of a plane? Only a *description* of the drawing will tell me that. Without a description I can only deduce what the figure *appears* to mean. Much easier to have 3-D models to explore with my hands.

But in this case, not possible. So I swept over the mishmash of ridges with both hands, redrew it with my ridging pen several times over, located the two triangles in it, and the lines connecting the two triangles' corners, and the lines made by extending the triangles' sides in one direction. I tried to make from my Taylor collection a 3-D model that accounted for the drawing—try that sometime, and understand how difficult this kind of intellectual feat can be. Projective imagination . . .

Certainly it seemed to be a rough sketch of Desargues's Theorem.

C. Desargues's Theorem was one of the first theorems clearly concerned with projective geometry; it was proposed by Girard Desargues in the mid-seventeenth century, in between his architectural and engineering efforts, his books on music, etc. It is a relatively simple theorem, in fact in three dimensions it is completely banal. Figure 1 describes it, refer back to it if you want; the theorem states that given the relationships shown in the diagram, points P, Q, and R will be collinear. The proof is simple indeed. By definition P, Q, and R lie on the same plane m as triangle ABC, and they lie on the same plane m' as A'B'C'. Two planes can only intersect in a line, and as P, Q, and R lie on both m and m' they must lie on that line of intersection. Therefore P, Q, and R are collinear, as was to be proved.

Obvious, you say, and it is true. But you would be surprised to learn how many proofs in geometry, when taken step by step and reduced to their constituent parts, are just as obvious. With a language so pure, things become clear. Would we had such a language for the heart.

It is also true, by the way, that this theorem is reciprocal: that is, if you postulate two triangles whose extensions of the sides meet at three collinear points, then it is possible to show that lines AA', BB', and CC' meet in a single point. As they say in the textbooks, I leave the proof of this as an exercise for the reader.

AC. But so what? I mean, it is a beautiful theorem, with the sort of purity and elegance characteristic of Renaissance math—but what was it doing in a drawing made by some poor prisoner of the Pentagon?

I considered this as I walked to my health club, Warren's Spa (considered it secondarily, anyway, and no doubt subconsciously; my primary concerns were the streets and the traffic. Washington's streets bear a certain resemblance to one of those confusing geometrical diagrams I described [the state streets crossing diagonally the regular gridwork, creating a variety of intersections]; happily one doesn't have to comprehend all the city at once to walk in it. But it is easy to become lost. So as I walked I concentrated on distances, on the sounds of the streets that tended to remain constant, on smells [the dirt of the park at M and New Hampshire, the hot-dog vendor on Twenty-first and K]; meanwhile my cane established the world directly before my feet, my sonar shades whistled rising or falling notes as objects approached or receded. . . . It takes some work just to get from point A to point B without getting disoriented [at which point one has to grind one's teeth and ask for directions] but it can be done, it is one of those small tasks/accomplishments [one chooses which, every time] that the blind cannot escape)—still, I did consider the matter of the drawing as I walked.

On H Street and Twenty-first I was pleased to smell the pretzel cart of my friend Ramon, who is also blind. His cart is the only one where the hot plate hasn't roasted several pretzels to that metallic burnt odor that all the other carts put off; Ramon prefers the clean smell of freshly baked dough, and he claims it brings him more customers, which I certainly believe. "Change only please," he was saying to someone briskly, "there's a change machine on the other side of the cart for your convenience, thanks. Hot pretzels! Hot pretzels, one dollar!"

"Hey there, Superblink!" I called as I approached him.

"Hey yourself, Professor Superblink," he replied. (Superblink is a mildly derogatory name used by irritated sighted social service people to describe those of their blind colleagues who are aggressively or ostentatiously competent in getting around, etc., who make a *display* of their competence. Naturally we have appreciated the term for our own use; sometimes it means the same thing for us—when used in the third person, usually—but in the second person it's a term of affection.) "Want a pretzel?"

"Sure."

"You off to the gym?"

"Yeah, I'm going to throw. Next time we play you're in trouble."

"That'll be the day, when my main mark starts beating me!"

I put four quarters in his callused hand and he gave me a pretzel. "Here's a puzzle for you," I said. "Why would someone try to convey a message by geometrical diagram?"

He laughed. "Don't ask me, that's your department!"

"But the message isn't for me."

"Are you sure about that?"

I frowned.

BC. At the health club I greeted Warren and Amanda at the front desk. They were laughing over a headline in the tabloid newspaper Amanda was shaking; they devoured those things, and pasted the best headlines all over the gym.

"What's the gem of the day?" I asked.

"How about 'Gay Bigfoot Molests Young Boys'?" Warren suggested.

"Or 'Woman Found Guilty of Turning Husband into Bank President,' " Amanda said, giggling. "She drugged him and did bemod to him until he went from teller to president."

Warren said, "I'll have to do that for you, eh Amanda?"

"Make me something better than a bank president."

Warren clicked his tongue. "Entirely too many designer drugs, these days. Come on, Carlos, I'll get the range turned on." I went to the locker room and changed, and when I got to the target room Warren was just done setting it up. "Ready to go," he said cheerily as he rolled past me.

I stepped in, closed the door, and walked out to the center of the room, where a waist-high wire column was filled with baseballs. I pulled out a baseball, hefted it, felt the stitching. A baseball is a beautiful object: nicely flared curves of the seams over the surface of a perfect sphere, an ideal object, exactly the right weight for throwing.

I turned on the range with a flick of a switch, and stepped away from the feeder, a ball in each hand. Now it was quite silent, only the slightest whirr faintly breathing through the soundproofed walls. I did what I could to reduce the sound of my own breathing, heard my heartbeat in my ears.

Then a *beep* behind me to my left, and low; I swirled and threw. Dull thud. "Right . . . low," said the machine voice from above, softly. *Beep* I threw again: "Right . . . high," it said louder, meaning I had missed by more. "Shit," I said as I got another two balls. "Bad start."

Beep—a hard throw to my left—*clang!* "Yeah!" There is very little in life more satisfying than the bell-like clanging of the target circle when hit square. It rings at about middle C with several overtones, like a small thick church bell hit with a hammer. The sound of success.

Seven more throws, four more hits. "Five for ten," the machine voice said. "Average strike time, one-point-three-five seconds. Fastest strike time, point-eight-four seconds."

Ramon sometimes hit the target in half a second or less, but I needed to hear the full beep to keep my average up. I set up for another round, pushed the button, got quiet, *beep* throw, *beep* throw, working to shift my feet faster, to follow through, to use the information from my misses to correct for the next time the target was near the floor, or the ceiling, or behind me (my weakness is the low ones, I can't seem to throw down accurately). And as I warmed up I threw harder and harder. Just throwing a baseball as hard as you can is a joy in itself. And then to set that bell ringing! *Clang!* It chimes every cell of you.

But when I quit and took a shower, and stood before my locker and reached in to free my shirt from a snag on the top of the door, my fingers brushed a small metal buttonlike thing stuck to an upper inside corner, where the door would usually conceal it from both me and my sighted companions; it came away when I pulled on it. I fingered it. The world is full of peculiar things. The cold touch of the unknown, so often felt . . . I am wary, I am always wary, I have to be wary.

I couldn't be certain what it was, but I had my suspicions, so I took it to my friend James Gold, who works in acoustics in the engineering department, and had him take a confidential look at it.

"It's a little remote microphone, all right," he said, and then joked: "Who's bugging you, Carlos?"

He got serious when I asked him where I could get a system like that for myself.

AB. "John Metcalf—'Blind Jack of Knaresborough'—(1717–1810). At six he lost his sight through small-pox, at nine he could get on pretty well unaided, at fourteen he announced his intention of disregarding his affliction thenceforward and of behaving in every respect as a normal human being. It is true that immediately on this brave resolve he fell into a gravel pit and received a serious hurt while escaping, under pursuit, from an orchard he was robbing ... fortunately this did not affect his self-reliance. At twenty he had made a reputation as a pugilist."(!)
> —Ernest Bramah, Introduction,
> *The Eyes of Max Carrados*

I have to fight, do you understand? The world wasn't made for me. Every day is fifteen rounds, a scramble to avoid being knocked flat, a counterpunch at every threatening sound.

When I was young I loved to read Ernest Bramah's stories about Max Carrados, the blind detective. Carrados could hear, smell, and feel with incredible sensitivity, and his ingenious deductions were never short of brilliant; he was fearless in a pinch; also, he was rich, and had a mansion, and a secretary, manservant, and chauffeur who acted as his eyes. All great stuff for the imaginative young reader, as certainly I was. I read every book I could get my hands on; the voice of my reading machine was more familiar to me than any human voice that I knew. Between that reading and my mathematical work, I could have easily withdrawn from the world of my own experience into Cutsforth's "verbal unreality," and babbled on like Helen Keller about the shapes of clouds and the colors of flowers and the like. The world become nothing but a series of texts; sounds kind of like deconstructionism, doesn't it? And of course at an older age I was enamored of the deconstructionists of the last century. The world as text. Husserl's *The Origin of Geometry* is twenty-two pages long, Derrida's *Introduction to the Origin of Geometry* is a hundred and fifty-three pages long—you can see why it would have appealed to me. If, as the deconstructionists seemed to say, the world is nothing but a collection of texts, and I can read, then I am not missing anything by being blind, am I?

The young can be very stubborn, very stupid.

AO. "All right, Jeremy," I said. "Let me meet this mysterious *subject* of yours who draws all this stuff."

"You want to?" he said, trying to conceal his excitement.

"Sure," I replied. "I'm not going to find out any more about all this until I do." My own subtext, yes; but I am better at hiding such things than Jeremy is.

"What have you found out? Do the diagrams mean anything to you?"

"Not much. You know me, Jeremy, drawings are my weakness. I'd rather have her do it in models, or writing, or verbally. You'll have to bring her by if you want me to continue."

"Well, okay. I'll see what I can do. She's not much help, though. You'll find out." But he was pleased.

BA. One time in high school I was walking out of the gym after PE, and I heard one of my coaches (one of the best teachers I have ever had) in his office, speaking to someone (he must have had his back to me)—he said, "You know, it's not the physical handicaps that will be the problem for most of these kids. It's the emotional problems that tend to come with the handicaps that will be the real burden for most of them."

OAA'. I was in my office listening to my reading machine. Its flat, uninflected mechanical voice (almost unintelligible to some of my colleagues) had over the years become a sort of helpless, stupid friend. I called it George, and was always programming into it another pronunciation rule to try to aid its poor speech, but to no avail; George always found new ways to butcher the language. I put the book face-down on the glass; "Finding first line," croaked George as the scanner inside the machine thumped around. Then it read from Roberto Torretti, a philosopher of geometry, quoting and discussing Ernst Mach. (Hear this spoken in the most stilted, awkward, syllable-by-syllable mispronunciation that you can imagine.)

"Mach says that our notions of space are rooted in our *physiological* constitution, and that geometric concepts are the product of the idealization of *physical* experiences of space." (George raises his voice in pitch to indicate italics, which also slow him down considerably.) "But physiological space is quite different from the infinite, isotropic, metric space of classical geometry and physics. It can, at most, be structured as a topological space. When viewed in this way, it naturally falls into several components: visual or optic space, tactile or haptic space, auditive space, etc. Optic space is anisotropic, finite, limited. Haptic space or the space of our skin, Mach says, corresponds to a two-dimensional, finite, unlimited (closed) Riemannian space. This is nonsense, for R-spaces are metric while haptic space is not. I take it that Mach means to say that haptic space can naturally be regarded as a two-dimensional compact connected topological space. But Mach does not emphasize enough the disconnectedness of haptic from optic space—"

There came four quick knocks at my door. I pressed the button on George that stopped him, and said, "Come in!"

The door opened. "Carlos!"

"Jeremy," I said. "How are you."

"Fine. I've brought Mary Unser with me—you know—the one who drew—"

I stood, feeling/hearing the presence of the other in the room. And there are times (like this one) when you *know* the other is in some odd, undefinable way, *different*, or . . . (Our language is not made for the experience of the blind. No words for this feeling, this apprehension.)

"I'm glad to meet you," I said.

I have said that I can tell dark from light, and I can, to an extent, though it is seldom very useful information. In this case, however, I was startled to have my attention drawn to my "sight"—for this woman was darker than other people, she was a sort of bundle of darkness in the room, her face distinctly lighter than the rest of her (or was that her face, exactly?).

A long pause. Then: "On border stand we n-dimensional space the," she said. Coming just after George's reading, I was struck by a certain similarity: the mechanical lilt from word to word; the basic incomprehension of a reading machine. . . . Goose bumps rose on my forearms.

Her voice itself, on the other hand, had George beat hands down. Fundamentally vibrant under the odd intonation, it was a voice with a very thick timbre, a bassoon or a hurdy-gurdy of a voice, with the buzz of someone who habitually speaks partly through the sinuses; this combined with overrelaxed vocal cords, what speech pathologists call *glottal fry*. Usually nasal voices are not pleasant, but pitch them low enough . . .

She spoke again, more slowly (definitely glottal fry): "We stand on the border of n-dimensional space."

"Hey," Jeremy said. "Pretty good!" He exclaimed: "Her word order isn't usually as . . . ordinary as that."

"So I gathered," I said. "Mary, what do you mean by that?"

"I—*oh*—" A kazoo squeak of distress, pain. I approached her, put out a hand. She took it as if to shake: a hand about the size of mine, narrow, strong fat muscle at base of thumb; trembling distinctly.

"I work on the geometries of topologically complex spaces," I said. "I am more likely than most to understand what you say."

"Are within never see we points us."

"That's true." But there was something wrong here, something I didn't like, though I couldn't tell exactly what it was. Had she spoken toward Jeremy? Speaking to me while she looked at him? The cold touch . . . a bundle of darkness in the dark . . . "But why are your sentences so disordered, Mary? Your words don't come out in the order you thought them. You must know that, since you understand us."

"Folded—*oh!*" Again the double-reed squeak, and suddenly she was weeping, trembling hard; we sat her down on my visitor's couch and Jeremy got her a glass of water, while she quaked in my hands. I stroked her hair (short, loosely curled, wild) and took the opportunity for a quick phrenological check: skull regular and as far as I could tell, undamaged; temples wide, distinct; same for eye sockets; nose a fairly ordinary pyramidal segment, no bridge to speak of; narrow cheeks, wet with tears. She reached up and took my right hand, and her little finger squeezed it hard, three times fast, three times slow, while she sobbed and sort of hiccuped words: "Pain it, station, I, oh, fold end, bright, light, space fold, oh, ohhh . . ."

Well, the direct question is not always the best way. Jeremy returned with a glass of water, and drinking some seemed to calm her. Jeremy said, "Perhaps we could try again later. Although—" He didn't seem very surprised.

"Sure," I said. "Listen, Mary, I'll talk to you again when you're feeling better."

But the language of touch, reduced to a simple code. SO . . . S?

OA. After Jeremy got her out of the office and disposed of her (how? with whom?) he returned to the seventh floor.

"So what the hell happened to her?" I asked angrily. "Why is she like that?"

"We aren't completely sure," he said slowly. "Here's why. She was one of the scientists staffing Tsiolkovsky Base Five, up in the mountains on the back side of the moon, you know. She's an astronomer and cosmologist. Well—I have to ask you to keep this quiet—one day Base Five stopped all broadcasting, and when they went over to see what was wrong, they found only her, wandering the station alone in a sort of catatonic state. No sign of the other scientists or station crew—eighteen people gone without a trace. And nothing much different to explain what had happened, either."

I *hmphed*. "What do they think happened?"

"They're still not sure. Apparently no one else was in the area, or could have been, et cetera. It's been suggested by the Russians, who had ten people there, that this could be first contact—you know, that aliens took the missing ones, and somehow disarranged Mary's thought processes, leaving her behind as a messenger that isn't working. Her brain scans are bizarre. I mean, it doesn't sound very likely—"

"No."

"But it's the only theory that explains everything they found there. Some of which they won't tell me about. So, we're doing what we can to get Mary's testimony, but as you can see, it's hard. She seems most comfortable drawing diagrams."

"Next time we'll start with that."

"Okay. Any other ideas?"

"No," I lied. "When can you bring her back again?"

AO. As if because I was blind I couldn't tell I was being duped!

Alone again, I struck fist into palm angrily. Oh, they were making a mistake, all right. They didn't know how much the voice reveals. The voice's secret expressivity reveals *so much!*— the language really is not adequate to tell it, we need that mathematics of emotion. . . . In the high school for the blind that I briefly attended for some of my classes, it often happened that a new teacher was instantly disliked, for some falseness in his or her voice, some quality of condescension or pity or self-congratulation that the teacher (and his or her superiors) thought completely concealed, if they knew of it at all. But it was entirely obvious to the students, because the voice is so utterly revealing, much more so I think than facial expressions; certainly it is less under our control. This is what makes most acting performances unsatisfactory to me; the vocal qualities are so stylized, so removed from those of real life. . . .

And here, I thought, I was witnessing a performance.

There is a moment in Olivier Messiaen's *Visions de l'Amen* when one piano is playing a progression of major chords, very traditionally harmonic, while on another piano high pairs of notes plonk down across the other's chords, ruining their harmony, crying out, Something's wrong! Something's wrong!

I sat at my desk and swayed side to side, living just such a moment. Something was wrong. Jeremy and this woman were lying, their voices said it in every intonation.

When I collected myself I called the department secretary, who had a view of the hall to the elevator. "Delphina, did Jeremy just leave?"

"Yes, Carlos. Do you want me to try and catch him?"

"No, I only need a book he left in his office. Can I borrow the master key and get it?"

"Okay."

I got the key, entered Jeremy's office, closed the door. One of the tiny pickups that James Gold had gotten for me fit right under the snap-in plug of the telephone cord. Then a microphone under the desk, behind a drawer. And out. (I have to be bold every day, you see, just to get by. I have to be wary, I have to be *bold*. But they didn't know that.)

Back in my office I closed and locked the door, and began to search. My office is big: two couches, several tall bookcases, my desk, a file cabinet, a coffee table. . . . When the partitions on the seventh floor of the Gelman Library were moved around to make more room, Delphina and George Hampton, who was chairman that year, had approached me nervously: "Carlos, you wouldn't mind an office with no windows, would you?"

I laughed. All of the full professors had offices on the outer perimeter of the floor, with windows.

"You see," George said, "since none of the windows in the building opens anyway, you won't be missing out on any breezes. And if you take this room in the inner core of the building, then we'll have enough space for a good faculty lounge."

"Fine," I said, not mentioning that I could see sunlight, distinguish light and dark. It made me angry that they hadn't remembered that, hadn't thought to ask. So I nicknamed my office "The Vault," and I had a lot of room, but no windows. The halls had no windows either, so I was really without sun, but I didn't complain.

Now I got down on hands and knees and continued searching, feeling like it was hopeless. But I found one, on the bottom of the couch. And there was another in the phone. Bugged. I left them in position and went home.

Home was a small top-floor apartment up near Twenty-first and N streets, and I supposed it was bugged too. I turned up Stockhausen's *Telemusik* as loud as I could stand it, hoping to drive my listeners into a suicidal fugal state, or at least give them a headache. Then I slapped together a sandwich, downed it angrily.

I imagined I was captain of a naval sailing ship (like Horatio Hornblower), and that because of my sharp awareness of the wind I was the best captain afloat. They had had to evacuate the city and all the people I knew were aboard, depending on me to save them. But we were caught against a lee shore by two large ships of the line, and in the ensuing broadsides (roar of cannon, smell of gunpowder and blood, screams of wounded like shrieking sea gulls), everyone I knew fell—chopped in half, speared by giant splinters, heads removed by cannon-ball, you name it. Then when they were all corpses on the sand-strewn splintered decking, I felt a final broadside discharge, every ball converging on me as if I were point O in figure 1. Instant dissolution and death.

I came out of it feeling faintly disgusted with myself. But Cutsforth says that because this type of fantasy in the blind subject actively defends the ego by eradicating those who attack its self-esteem, it is a healthy thing. (At least in fourteen-year-olds.) So be it. Here's to health. Fuck all of you.

C. Geometry is a language, with a vocabulary and syntax as clear and precise as humans can make them. In many cases definitions of terms and operations are explicitly spelled out, to help achieve this clarity. For instance, one could say:

Let (parentheses) designate additional information.

Let [brackets] designate secret causes.

Let {braces} designate . . .

But would it be true, in this other language of the heart?

AB. Next afternoon I played beepball with my team. Sun hot on my face and arms, spring smell of pollen and wet grass. Ramon got six runs in the at-bat before mine (beepball is a sort of cricket/softball mix, played with softball equipment ["It shows you can play cricket blind" one Anglophobe {she was Irish} said to me once]), and when I got up I scratched out two and then struck out. Swinging *too* hard. I decided I liked outfield better. The beepball off in the distance, lofted up in a short arc, smack of bat, follow the ball up and up—out toward me!—drift in its direction, the rush of fear, glove before face as it approaches, stab for it, off after it as it rolls by—pick it up—Ramon's voice calling clearly, "Right here! Right here!"—and letting loose with a throw—really putting everything into it—and then, sometimes, hearing that beepball lance off into the distance and smack into Ramon's glove. It was great. Nothing like outfield.

And next inning I hit one *hard*, and that's great too. A counterpunch. That feeling goes right up your arms and all through you.

Walking home I brooded over Max Carrados, blind detective, and over Horatio Hornblower, sighted naval captain. Over Thomas Gore, blind senator from Oklahoma. As a boy his fantasy was to become a senator. He read the *Congressional Record*, joined the debate team, organized his whole life around the project. And he became senator. I knew that sort of fantasy as well as I knew the vengeful adolescent daydreams: all through my youth I dreamed of being a mathematician. And here I was. So one could do it. One could imagine doing something, and then do it.

But that meant that one had, by definition, imagined something *possible*. And one couldn't always say ahead of the attempt whether one had imagined the possible or the impossible. And even if one had imagined something possible, that didn't guarantee a successful execution of the plan.

The team we had played was called "Helen Keller Jokes" (there are some good ones, too [they come {of course} from Australia] but I won't go into that). It's sad that such an intelligent woman was so miseducated—not so much by Sullivan as by her whole era: all that treacly Victorian sentimentality poured into her, "The fishing villages of Cornwall are very picturesque, seen either from the beaches or the hilltops, with all their boats riding to their moorings or sailing about in the harbor—When the moon, large and serene, floats up the sky, leaving in the water a long track of brightness like a plow breaking up a soil of silver, I can only sigh my ecstasy," come on, Helen. Get off it. Now that is living in a world of texts.

But didn't I live most (all?) of my life in texts as least as unreal to me as moonlight on water was to Helen Keller? These n-dimensional manifolds I had explored for so long . . . I suppose the basis for my abilities in them was the lived reality of haptic space, but still, it was many removes from my actual experience. And so was the situation I found myself confronted with now, Jeremy and Mary acting out some drama I did not comprehend. And so was my plan to deal with it. Verbalism, words versus reality . . .

I caressed my glove, refelt the shiver of bat against beepball. Brooded anxiously over my plan. Under attack, disoriented, frightened. For months after my mother left I made plans to get her back. I invented ailments, I injured myself, I tried to slip away and fly to Mexico. Why had she gone? It was inconceivable. Father didn't want to speak of it. They didn't love each other anymore, he said once. It was hard for her, she didn't speak the language. They wouldn't let her stay as a single person. She

couldn't take care of me in Mexico, she had
family burdens, things were bad there, and besides he didn't want me to leave, he was my
principal teacher now, my caretaker. None of
it meant anything to me. I barely even heard
him. A whole language of hands, lost. I began
to forget and clasped my own hands together
and made the words, forefingers for food, the
outdoor squeeze, the wanting sweep, the pressure that said I love you. No one heard.

OAA′. The next time Jeremy brought Mary
Unser by my office, I said very little. I got out
my visitor's supply of paper and pencils, and
set her down at the coffee table. I brought over
my models: subatomic particles breaking up in
a spray of wire lines, like water out of a shower
head; strawlike Taylor sticks for model making; polyhedric blocks of every kind. I sat down
with the ridged sheets made from her earlier
drawings, and the models I had attempted to
make of them, and I started asking very limited
questions. "What does this line mean? Does it
go before or behind? Is this R or R'? Have I
got this right?"

And she would honk a sort of laugh, or say
"No, no, no, no," (no problem with sequencing
there) and draw furiously. I took the pages as
she finished them and put them in my xerox,
took out the ridged, bumpy sheets and had her
guide my fingers over them. Even so they were
difficult, and with a squeak of frustration she

went to the straw models, clicking together triangles, parallels, etc. This was easier, but eventually she reached a limit here, too. "Need drawing beyond," she said.

"Fine. Write down whatever you want."

She wrote, and then read aloud to me, or I put it through my xerox machine marked "translation to Braille." And we forged on, with Jeremy looking over our shoulders the whole time.

And eventually we came very close to the edge of my work. (The cold touch.) Following subatomic particles down into the microdimensions where they appeared to make their "jumps." I had proposed an n-dimensional topological manifold, where $1 < n < $ infinity, so that the continuum being mapped fluctuated between one and some finite number of dimensions, going from a curving line to a sort of n-dimensional Swiss cheese, if you like, depending on the amounts of energy displayed in the area in any of the four forms, electromagnetism, gravity, or the strong and weak interactions. The geometry for this manifold pattern (so close to the experience of haptic space) had, as I have said, attracted the attention of physicists at CERN and SLAC—but there were still unexplained areas, as far as I could tell, and the truth was *I had not published this work.*

So here I was "conversing" with a young woman who in ordinary conversations could not order her words correctly—who in this realm spoke with perfect coherence—who was in fact speaking about (inquiring about?) the edges of my own private work.

The kind of work that Jeremy Blasingame used to ask me about so curiously.

I sighed. We had been going on for two or three hours, and I sat back on the couch. My hand was taken up in Mary's, given a reassuring squeeze. I didn't know what to make of it. "I'm tired," I said.

"I feel better," she said. "Easier to talk way—this way."

"Ah," I said. I took up the model of a positron hitting a "stationary" muon: a wire tree, trunk suddenly bursting into a mass of curling branches. . . . So it was here: one set of events, a whole scattering of explanations. Still, the bulk of the particles shot out in a single general direction (the truths of haptic space).

She let go of my hand to make one last diagram. Then she xeroxed it for me, and guided my hands over the ridged copy.

Once again it was Desargues's Theorem: triangles ABC and A′B′C′, projected from point O. Only this time the two triangles were in the same plane, and AB and A′B′ were parallel, as were BC and B′C′, and AC and A′C′. P, Q, and R had become ideal points; and she put my finger in the areas marking these ideal points, time after time.

* * *

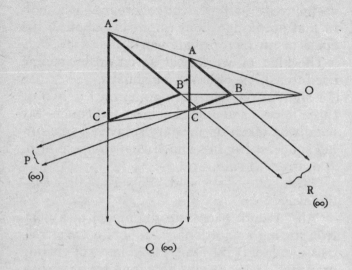

Figure 2

C. Perhaps I should explain a little further, for now we leave the Euclidean world behind.

The geometry of ordinary points and lines (Euclidean geometry) is greatly complicated by the fact that a pair of parallel lines do not meet in a point. Why should this be so? Altering Euclid's fifth axiom concerning parallels led to the first non-Euclidean geometries of Lobachevski and Bolyai and Riemann. To enter this altered world we only need to add to the ordinary points on each line a single "ideal" point. This point belongs to all lines parallel to the given line. Now every pair of lines in the plane will intersect in a single point; lines not parallel will intersect in an ordinary point, and lines parallel will intersect in the ideal point common to the two lines. For intuitive reasons the ideal point is called the *point at infinity* on the line.

(This notion of ideality can be extended to other geometrical figures: all the points at infinity in a plane lie on a *line at infinity;* all the lines at infinity lie on the *plane at infinity,* the ideal plane in space, out beyond the rest; and all ideal planes lie in the *space at infinity,* in the next dimension over; and so on, unto *n* dimensions. [In the haptic space of Nevskyan geometry I can feel the presence of these ideal realms, for beyond certain ideal planes {membranes just beyond my touch} there are ideal activities that I can only imagine, can only yearn for. . . .])

Note, by the way, that with the concept of ideal points we can prove Desargues's Theorem in a single plane. Remember that to prove a theorem in general it suffices to prove it in a special case, as here, where AB and A′B′ are parallel, and the same for BC and B′C′, and AC and A′C′. As these pairs of lines are parallel, they intersect at their ideal points—call them P, Q, and R again for familiarity. And since all ideal points in a plane lie on the line at infinity, then P, Q, and R are collinear. Simple. And this proves not only the specific case when the sides of the triangles are parallel, but all the other cases, when they are not.

If only the world conformed to this rigorous logic!

A'AO. At this point Mary said, "Mr. Blasingame, I need a drink of water." He went out to the hall water dispenser, and she quickly took my forefinger between her finger and thumb (pads flattening with an inappropriate pressure, until my finger ached)—squeezed twice, and jabbed my finger first onto her leg, then onto the diagram, tracing out one of the triangles. She repeated the movements, then poked my leg and traced out the other triangle. Fine; she was one, I was the other. We were parallel, and in projection from point O, which was . . .

But she only traced the lines to point O, over and over. What did she mean?

Jeremy returned, and she let my hand go. Then in a while, after the amenities (hard handshake, quivering hand) Jeremy whisked her off.

When he returned, I said, "Jeremy, is there any chance I can talk to her alone? I think she's made nervous by your presence—the associations, you know. She really does have an interesting perspective on the n-dimensional manifold, but she gets confused when she stops and interacts with you. I'd just like to take her for a walk, you know—down by the canal, or the Tidal Basin, perhaps, and talk things over with her. It might get the results you want."

"I'll see what they say," Jeremy said in an expressionless voice.

That night I put on a pair of earplugs, and played the tape of Jeremy's phone conversations. In one when the phone was picked up he said:

"He wants to talk with her alone now."

"Fine," said a tenor voice. "She's prepared for that."

"This weekend?"

"If he agrees." *Click.*

BA. I listen to music. I listen to twentieth-century composers the most, because many of them made their music out of the sounds of the world we live in now, the world of jets and sirens and industrial machinery, as well as bird song and wood block and the human voice. Messiaen, Partch, Reich, Glass, Shapiro, Subotnik, Ligeti, Penderecki—these first explorers away from the orchestra and the classical tradition remain for me the voices of our age. They speak to me. In fact they speak for me; in their dissonance and confusion and anger I hear myself being expressed, I hear the loss and feel its transformation into something else, into something less painful. And so I listen to their difficult, complex music because I understand it, which gives me pleasure, and because while doing I am participating fully, I am excelling. No one can bring more to the act than I. I am *in control*.

I listened to music.

O. You see, these *n*-dimensional manifolds ... if we understood them well enough to manipulate them, to tap their energy ... well, there is a tremendous amount of energy contained there. That kind of energy means power, and power ... draws the powerful. Or those seeking power, fighting for it. I began to feel the extent of the danger.

BB′. She was quiet as we walked across the Mall toward the Lincoln Monument. I think she would have stopped me if I had spoken about anything important. But I knew enough to say nothing, and I think she guessed I knew she was bugged. I held the back of her upper arm loosely in my left hand, and let her guide us. A sunny, windy day, with occasional clouds obscuring the sun for a minute or two. Down by the Mall's lake the slightly stagnant smell of wet algae tinged all the other scents: grass, dust, the double strand of lighter fluid and cooking meat.... The sink of darkness swirling around the Vietnam Memorial. Pigeons cooed their weird, larger-than-life coos, and flapped away noisily as we walked through their affairs. We sat on grass that had been recently cut, and I brushed a hand over the stiff blades.

A curious procedure, this conversation. No visuals, for me; and perhaps we were being watched, as well. (Such a common anxiety of the blind, the fear of being watched—and here it was true.) And we couldn't talk freely, even though at the same time we had to say something, to keep Blasingame and friends from thinking I was aware of anything wrong. "Nice day." "Yeah. I'd love to be out on the water on a day like this." "Really?" "Yeah."

And all the while two fingers held one finger. My hands are my eyes, and always have been. Now they were as expressive as voice, as receptive as ever touch can be, and into haptic space we projected a conversation of rare urgency. Are you okay? I'm okay. Do you know what's going on? Not entirely, can't explain.

"Let's walk down to the paddle boats and go out on the Basin, then."

I said, "Your speech is much better today."

She squeezed my hand thrice, hard. False information? "I . . . had . . . electroshock." Her voice slid, slurred; it wasn't entirely under control.

"It seems to have helped."

"Yes. Sometimes."

"And the ordering of your mathematical thought?"

Buzzing laugh, hurdy-gurdy voice: "I don't know—more disarranged, perhaps—complementary procedure? You'll have to tell me."

"As a cosmologist did you work in this area?"

"The topology of the microdimensions apparently determines both gravity and the weak interaction, wouldn't you agree?"

"I couldn't say. I'm not much of a physicist."

Three squeezes again. "But you must have an idea or two about it?"

"Not really? You?"

"Perhaps ... once. But it seems to me your work is directly concerned with it."

"Not that I know of."

Stalemate. Was that right? I was becoming more and more curious about this woman, whose signals to me were so mixed. ... Once again she seemed a bundling of darkness in the day, a whirlpool where all lightness disappeared, except for around her head. (I suppose I imagine all that I "see," I suppose they are always haptic visions.)

"Are you wearing dark clothes?"

"Not really. Red, beige ..."

As we walked I held her arm more tightly. She was about my height. Her arm muscles were distinct, and her lats pushed out from her ribs. "You must swim."

"Weight lifting, I'm afraid. They made us on Luna."

"On Luna," I repeated.

"Yes," and she fell silent.

This really was impossible. I didn't think she was completely an ally—in fact I thought she was lying—but I felt an underlying sympathy from her, and a sense of conspiracy with her, that grew more powerful the longer we were together. The problem was, what did that feeling mean? Without the ability to converse freely, I was stymied in my attempts to learn more; pushed this way and that in the crosscurrents of her behavior, I could only wonder what she was thinking. And what our listeners made of this mostly silent day in the sun.

So we paddled out onto the Tidal Basin, and talked from time to time about the scene around us. I love the feel of being on water—the gentle rocking over other boats' wakes, the wet stale smell. . . . "Are the cherry trees blossoming still?"

"Oh yes. Not quite at the peak, but just past. It's beautiful. Here—" she leaned out—"here's one about to drown." She put it in my hand. I sniffed at it. "Do they smell?"

"No, not much," I said. "The prettier people say flowers are, the less scent they seem to have. Did you ever notice that?"

"I guess. I like the scent of roses."

"It's faint, though. These blossoms must be very beautiful—they smell hardly at all."

"En masse they are lovely. I wish you could see them."

I shrugged. "And I wish you could touch their petals, or feel us bouncing about as I do. I have enough sense data to keep entertained."

"Yes . . . I suppose you do." She left her hand

covering mine. "I suppose we're out quite a ways," I said. So that we couldn't be seen well from the shore, I meant.

"From the dock, anyway. We're actually almost across the Basin."

I moved my hand from under hers, and held her shoulder. Deep hollow behind her collarbone. This contact, this conversation of touch . . . it was most expressive hand to hand, and so I took her hand again, and our fingers made random entanglements, explorations. Children shouting, then laughing in boats to our left, voices charged with excitement. How to speak in this language of touch?

Well, we all know that. Fingertips, brushing lines of the palm; ruffling the fine hair at the back of the wrist; fingers pressing each other back: these are sentences, certainly. And it is a difficult language to lie in. That catlike sensuous stretch, under my stroking fingertips . . .

"We've got a clear run ahead of us," she said after a time, voice charged with humming overtones.

"Stoke the furnaces," I cried. "Damn the torpedoes!" And with a gurgling *clug-clug-clug-clug* we paddle-wheeled over the Basin into the fresh wet wind, sun on our faces, laughing at the release from tension (bassoon and baritone), crying out "Mark twain!" or "Snag dead ahead" in jocular tones, entwined hands crushing the other as we pedaled harder and harder . . . "Down the Potomac!" "Across the sea!" and the spray cold on the breeze—

She stopped pedaling, and we swerved left.

"We're almost back," she said quietly.

We let the boat drift in, without a word.

OA. My bugs told me that my office had been broken into, by two, possibly three people, only one of whom spoke—a man, in an undertone: "Try the file cabinet." The cabinet drawers were rolled out (familiar clicking of the runners over the ball bearings), and the desk drawers, too, and then there was the sound of paper shuffling, of things being knocked about.

I also got an interesting phone conversation over Jeremy's phone. The call was incoming; Jeremy said "Yes?" and a male voice—the same one Jeremy had called earlier—said, "She says he's unwilling to go into any detail."

"That doesn't surprise me," Jeremy said. "But I'm sure he's got—"

"Yes, I know. Go ahead and try what we discussed."

The break-in, I supposed.

"Okay." *Click.*

AO. No doubt it never even occurred to them that I might turn the tables on them, or act against them in any way, or even figure out that something was strange. It made me furious.

* * *

OA. At the same time I was frightened. You feel the lines of force, living in Washington, D.C.; feel the struggle for power among the shadowy manifolds surrounding the official government space; read of the unsolved murders, of shadowy people whose jobs are not made clear. . . . As a blind person one feels apart from that nebulous world of intrigue and hidden force, on the edge by reason of disability. ("No one harms a blind man.") Now I knew I was part of it, pulled in, on my own. It was frightening.

But they didn't know how much I knew. Snuffle of an approaching boxer, counterpunch right in the face. I have to be bold just to cross the street!

AA'. One night I was immersed in Harry Partch's *Cloud Chamber Music*, floating in those big glassy notes, when my doorbell rang. I picked up the phone. "Hello?"

"It's Mary Unser. May I come up?"

"Sure." I pushed the button and walked onto the landing.

She came up the stairs alone. "Sorry to bother you at home," she buzzed, out of breath. Such a voice. "I looked up your address in the phone book. I'm not supposed . . ."

She stood before me, touched my right arm. I lifted my hand and held her elbow. "Yes?"

Nervous, resonant laugh. "I'm not supposed to be here."

Then you'll soon be in trouble, I wanted to
say. But surely she knew my apartment would
be bugged? Surely she *was* supposed to be
here? She was trembling violently, enough so
that I put up my other hand and held her by
the shoulders. "Are you all right?"

"Yes. No." Falling oboe tones, laugh that was
not a laugh ... She seemed frightened, very
frightened. I thought, if she is acting she is *very*
good.

"Come on in," I said, and led her inside. I
went to the stereo and turned down the
Partch—then reconsidered, and turned it back
up. "Have a seat—the couch is nice." I was nervous myself. "Would you like something to
drink?" Quite suddenly it all seemed unreal, a
dream, one of my fantasies. Phantasmagoric
cloud chamber ringing to things, how did I
know what was real? Those membranes. Beyond the plane at infinity, what?

"No. Or yes." She laughed again, that laugh
that was not a laugh.

"I've got some beer." I went to the refriger-
ator, got a couple of bottles, opened them.

"So what's going on?" I said as I sat down
beside her. As she spoke I drank from my beer,
and she stopped from time to time to take long
swallows.

"Well, I feel that the more I understand what
you're saying about the transfer of energies between n-dimensional manifolds, the better I
understand what ... happened to me." But now

there was a different sound to her voice—an overtone was gone, it was less resonant, less nasal.

I said, "I don't know what I can tell you. It's not something I can talk about, or even write down. What I can express, I have, you know. In papers." This a bit louder, for the benefit of our audience. (If there was one?)

"Well . . ." and her hand, under mine, began to tremble again.

We sat there for a very long time, and all during that time we conversed through those two hands, saying things I can scarcely recall now, because we have no language for that sort of thing. But they were important things nevertheless, and after a while I said, "Here. Come with me. I'm on the top floor, so I have a sort of a porch on the roof. Finish your beer. It's a pleasant night out, you'll feel better outside." I led her through the kitchen to the pantry, where the door to the backstairs was. "Go on up." I went back to the stereo and put on Jarrett's *Köln Concert*, loud enough so we'd be able to hear it. Then I went up the stairs onto the roof, and crunched over the tarred gravel.

This was one of my favorite places. The sides of the building came up to the chest around the edge of the roof, and on two sides large willows draped their branches over it, making it a sort of haven. I had set a big old wreck of a couch out there, and on certain nights when the wind was up and the air was cool, I would lie back on it with a bumpy Braille planisphere in my hands, listening to Scholz's *Starcharts* and feeling that with those projections I knew what it was to see the night sky.

"This is nice," she said.

"Isn't it?" I pulled the plastic sheet from the couch, and we sat.

"Carlos?"

"Yes?"

"I—I—" That double-reed squeak—

I put an arm around her. "Please," I said, suddenly upset myself. "Not now. Not now. Just relax. Please." And she turned into me, her head rested on my shoulder; she trembled. I dug my fingers into her hair and slowly pulled them through the tangles. Shoulder length, no more. I cupped her ears, stroked her neck. She calmed.

Time passed, and I only caressed. No other thought, no other perception. How long this went on I couldn't say—perhaps a half hour? Perhaps longer. She made a sort of purring kazoo sound, and I leaned forward and kissed her. Jarrett's voice, crying out briefly over a fluid run of piano notes. She pulled me to her, her breath caught, rushed out of her. The kiss became intense, tongues dancing together in a whole intercourse of their own, which I felt all through me in that *chakra* way, neck, spine, belly, groin, nothing but kiss. And without the slightest bit of either intention or resistance, I fell into it.

I remember a college friend once asked me, hesitantly, if I didn't have trouble with my love life. "Isn't it hard to tell when they . . . want to?" I had laughed. The whole process, I had wanted to say, was amazingly easy. The blind's dependence on touch puts them in an advance position, so to speak: using hands to see faces, being led by the hand (being dependent), one has already crossed what Russ calls the border between the world of not-sex and the world of sex; once over that border (with an other feeling protective) . . .

My hands explored her body, discovering it then and there for the first time: as intensely exciting a moment as there is, in the whole process. I suppose I expect narrow-cheeked people to be narrow-hipped (it's mostly true, you'll find), but it wasn't so, in this case—her hips flared in those feminine curves that one can only hold, without ever getting used to (without ever [the otherness of the other] quite believing). On their own my fingers slipped under clothes, between buttons, as adroit as little mice, clever lusty little creatures, unbuttoning blouse, reaching behind to undo bra with a twist. She shrugged out of them both and I felt the softness of her breasts while she tugged at my belt. I shifted, rolled, put my ear to her hard sternum, kissing the inside of one breast as it pressed against my face, feeling that quick heartbeat speak to me. . . . She moved me back, got me unzipped, we paused for a speedy moment and got the rest of our clothes off, fumbling at our own and each other's until they were clear. Then it was flesh to flesh, skin to skin, in a single haptic space jumping with energy, with the insistent *yes* of caresses, mouth to mouth, four hands full, body to body, with breasts and erect penis crushed, as it were, between two pulsing walls of muscle.

The skin is the ultimate voice.

So we made love. As we did (my feet jabbing the end of the couch, which was quite broad enough, but a little too short) I arched up and let the breeze between us (cool on our sweat), leaned down and sucked on first one nipple and then the other—

(thus becoming helpless in a sense, a needy infant, completely dependent [because for the blind from birth, mother love is even more crucial than for the rest of us—the blind depend on their mothers for almost *everything*, for the sense of object permanence, for the education that makes the distinction between self and world, for the beginning of language, and also for the establishment of a private language that compensates for the lack of sight {if your mother doesn't know that a sweeping hand means *"I want!"*} and bridges the way to the common tongue—without all that, which only a mother can give, the blind infant is lost— without mother love beyond mother love, the blind child will very likely go mad] so that [for any of us] to suck on a lover's nipple brings

back that primal world of trust and need, I am
sure of it)

—I was sure of it even then, as I made love
to this strange other Mary Unser, a woman as
unknown to me as any I had ever spoken with.
At least until now. Now with each plunge into
her (cylinder capped by cone, sliding through
cylinder into rough sphere, neuron to neuron,
millions of them fusing across, so that I could
not tell where I stopped and she began) I
learned more about her, the shape of her, her
rhythms, her whole nerve-reality, spoken to me
in movement and touch (spread hands holding
my back, flanks, bottom) and in those broken
bassoon tones that were like someone humming, briefly, involuntarily. "Ah," I said happily at all this sensation, all this new
knowledge, feeling all my skin and all my
nerves swirl up like a gust of wind into my
spine, the back of my balls, to pitch into her
all my self—

When we were done (oboe squeaks) I slid
down, bending my knees so my feet stuck up
in the air. I wiggled my toes in the breeze. Faint
traffic noises played a sort of city music to ac-
company the piano in the apartment. From the
airshaft came the sound of a chorus of pigeons,
sounding like monkeys with their jaws wired
shut, trying to chatter. Mary's skin was damp
and I licked it, loving the salt. Patch of darkness in my blur of vision, darkness bundling in
it. . . . She rolled onto her side and my hands

played over her. Her biceps made a smooth hard bulge. There were several moles on her back, like little raisins half-buried in her skin. I pushed them down, fingered the knobs of her spine. The muscles of her back put her spine in a deep trough of flesh. Women are so bifurcated that way: between the shoulder blades the spine drops into a valley between two ridges of muscle, then dives even deeper between the halves of the butt, past the curl of the coccyx, past anus and vagina and the split nest of pubic hair and over the pubic bone, a sort of low pass; then on most women the valley begins again, as a broad depression up to belly button and up to sternum, and between breasts, and all the way up to the hollow between the collarbones, so that their whole torso is divided this way, into left and right. I explored this valley in Mary's body and she shifted, threw her top leg over mine. My head rested on her biceps, snuggled against her side.

I remembered a day my blind science class was taken to a museum, where we were allowed to feel a skeleton. All those hard bones, in just the right places; it made perfect sense, it was exactly as it felt under skin, really— there were no big surprises. But I remember being so upset by the experience of feeling the skeleton that I had to go outside and sit down on the museum steps. I don't know to this day exactly why I was so shaken, but I suppose (all those hard things left behind) it was something like this: it was frightening to know how *real* we were!

Now I tugged at her, gently. "Who are you, then."

"Not now." And as I started to speak again she put a finger to my mouth (scent of us): "A friend." Buzzing nasal whisper, like a tuning fork, like a voice I was beginning (and this scared me, for I knew I did not know her) to love: "A friend . . ."

C. At a certain point in geometrical thinking vision becomes only an obstruction. Those used to visualizing theorems (as in Euclidean geometry) reach a point, in the *n*-dimensional manifolds or elsewhere, where the concepts simply *can't* be visualized; and the attempt to do so only leads to confusion and misunderstanding. Beyond that point an interior geometry, a haptic geometry, guided by a kinetic aesthetics, is probably the best sensory analogy we have; and so I have my advantage.

But in the real world, in the geometries of the heart, do I ever have any comparable advantage? Are there things we feel that can never be seen?

OA. The central problem for everyone concerned with the relationship between geometry and the real world is the question of how one moves from the incommunicable impressions of the sensory world (vague fields of force, of danger), to the generally agreed-upon abstractions of the math (the explanation). Or, as Edmund Husserl puts it in *The Origin of Geometry* (and on this particular morning George was enunciating this passage for me with the utmost awkwardness): "How does geometrical ideality (just like that of all the sciences) proceed from its primary intrapersonal origin, where it is a structure within the conscious space of the first inventor's soul, to its ideal objectivity?"

At this point Jeremy knocked at my door: four quick raps. "Come in, Jeremy," I said, my pulse quickening.

He opened the door and looked in. "I have a pot of coffee just ready to go," he said. "Come on down and have some."

So I joined him in his office, which smelled wonderfully of strong French roast. I sat in one of the plush armchairs that circled Jeremy's desk, accepted a small glazed cup, sipped from it. Jeremy moved about the room restlessly as he chattered about one minor matter after another, obviously avoiding the topic of Mary, and all that she represented. The coffee sent a warm flush through me—even the flesh of my feet buzzed with heat, though in the blast of air-conditioned air from the ceiling vent I didn't start to sweat. At first it was a comfortable, even pleasant sensation. The bitter, murky taste of the coffee washed over my palate, through the roof of my mouth into my sinuses, from there up behind my eyes, through my brain, all the way down my throat, into my lungs: I breathed coffee, my blood singing with warmth.

... I had been talking about something. Jeremy's voice came from directly above and before me, and it had a crackly, tinny quality to it, as if made by an old carbon microphone: "And what would happen if the Q energy from this manifold were directed through these vectored dimensions into the macrodimensional manifold?"

Happily I babbled, "Well, provide each point P of an n-dimensional differentiable manifold M with the analogue of a tangent plane, an n-dimensional vector space Tp(M), called the tangent space at P. Now we can define a *path* in manifold M as a differentiable mapping of an open interval of R into M. And along this path we can fit the *whole* of the forces defining K the submanifold of M, a lot of energy to be sure," oh, yes, a lot of energy, and I was writing it all down, when the somatic effect of the drug caught up with the mental effect, and I recognized what was happening. ("Entirely too many new designer drugs these days. . . .")

Jeremy's breathing snagged as he looked up to see what had stopped me; meanwhile I struggled with a slight wave of nausea, caused more by the realization that I had been drugged than by the chemicals themselves, which had very little noise. What had I told him? And why, for God's sake, did it matter so much?

"Sorry," I muttered through the roar of the ventilator. "Bit of a headache."

"Sorry to hear that," Jeremy said, in a voice exactly like George's. "You look a little pale."

"Yes," I said, trying to conceal my anger. (Later, listening to the tape of the conversation, I thought I only sounded confused.) (And I hadn't said much about my work, either— mostly definitions.) "Sorry to run out on you, but it really is bothering me."

I stood, and for a moment I panicked; the location of the room's door—the most fundamental point of orientation, remembered without effort in every circumstance—wouldn't come to me. I was damned if I would ask Jeremy Blasingame about such a thing, or stumble about in front of him. I consciously fought to remember: desk faces door, chair faces desk, door therefore behind you. . . .

"Let me walk you to your office," Jeremy said, taking me by the arm. "Listen, maybe I can give you a lift home?"

"That's all right," I said, shrugging him off. I found the door by accident, it seemed, and left him. Down to my office, wondering if I would get the right door. My blood was hot Turkish coffee. My head spun. The key worked, so I had found the right door. Locked in I went to my couch and lay down. I was as dizzy there as standing, but found I couldn't move again. I spun in place helplessly. I had read that the drugs used for such purposes had almost no somatic effect, but perhaps this was true only for subjects less sensitive to their kinetic reality—otherwise, why was I reacting so? Fear. Or Jeremy had put something beyond the truth drug in me. A warning? Against? Suddenly I was aware of the tight boundaries of my comprehension, beyond it the wide manifold of action I did not understand—and the latter threatened to completely flood the former, so that there would be left nothing at all that I understood about this matter. Drowned in the unknown, ah, God, such a prospect terrified me!

Sometime later—perhaps as much as an hour—I felt I had to get home. Physically I felt much better, and it was only when I got outside in the wind that I realized that the psychological effects of the drug were still having their way with me. Rare, heavy waft of diesel exhaust, a person wearing clothes rank with old sweat: these smells overwhelmed any chance I had of locating Ramon's cart by nose. My cane felt unusually long, and the rising and falling whistles of my sonar glasses made a musical composition like something out of Messiaen's *Catalogue d'Oiseaux*. I stood entranced by the effect. Cars zoomed past with their electric whirrs, the wind made more sound than I could process. I couldn't find Ramon and decided to give up trying; it would be bad to get him mixed up in any of this anyway. Ramon was my best friend. All those hours at Warren's throwing together, and when we played beeper Ping-Pong at his apartment we sometimes got to laughing so hard we couldn't stand—and what else is friendship than that, after all?

Distracted by thoughts such as these, and by the bizarre music of wind and traffic, I lost track of which street I was crossing. The *whoosh* of a car nearly brushing me as I stepped up from a curb. Lost! "Excuse me, is this Pennsylvania or K?" Fuckyouverymuch. Threading my way fearfully between broken bottles, punji-stick nails poking up out of boards on the sidewalk, low-hanging wires holding up tree branch or street sign, dogshit on the curb waiting like banana peel to skid me into the street under a bus, speeding cars with completely silent electric motors careening around the corner, muggers who didn't care if I was blind or paraplegic or whatever, open manholes in the crosswalks, rabid dogs with their toothy jaws stuck out between the rails of a fence, ready to bite . . . Oh yes, I fought off all these dangers and more, and I must have looked mad tiptoeing down the sidewalk, whapping my cane about like a man beating off devils.

AO. By the time I got into my apartment I was shaking with fury. I turned on Steve

Reich's *Come Out* (in which the phrase "Come out to show them" is looped countless times) as loud as I could stand it, and barged around my place alternately cursing and crying (that stinging of the eyes), all under the sound of the music. I formulated a hundred impossible plans of revenge against Jeremy Blasingame and his shadowy employers, brushed my teeth for fifteen minutes to get the taste of coffee out of my mouth.

By the next morning I had a plan: it was time for some confrontation. It was a Saturday and I was able to work in my office without interruption. I entered the office and unlocked a briefcase, opened my file cabinet and made sounds of moving papers from briefcase to cabinet. Much more silently I got out a big mousetrap that I had bought that morning. On the back of it I wrote, *You're caught. The next trap kills.* I set the trap and placed it carefully behind the new file I had added to the cabinet. This was straight out of one of my adolescent rage fantasies, of course, but I didn't care, it was the best way I could think of to both punish them and warn them from a distance. When the file was pulled from the cabinet, the trap would release onto the hand pulling the file out, and it would also break tape set in a pattern only I would be able to feel. So if the trap went off, I would know.

The first step was ready.

* * *

CA. In Penderecki's *Threnody for the Victims of Hiroshima*, a moment of deadly stillness, strings humming dissonant strokes as the whole world waits.

Cut shaving; the smell of blood.

Across the road, a carpenter hammering nails on a roof, each set of seven strokes a crescendo: *tap-tap-tap-tap-tap-tap-TAP! Tap-tap-tap-tap-tap-tap-TAP!*

In that mathematics of emotion, stress calculations to measure one's tension: already there for us to use. Perhaps all of math already charts states of consciousness, moments of being.

CC'. She came to me again late at night, with the wind swirling by her through the doorway. It was late, the wind was chill and blustery, the barometer was falling. Storm coming.

"I wanted to see you," she said.

I felt a great thrill of fear, and another of pleasure, and I could not tell which was stronger or, after a time, which was which.

"Good." We entered the kitchen, I served her water, circled her unsteadily, my voice calm as we discussed trivia in fits and starts. After many minutes of this I very firmly took her by the hand. "Come along." I led her into the pantry, up the narrow musty stairs, out the roof door into the wind. A spattering of big raindrops hit us. "Carlos—" "Never mind that!" The *whoosh* of the wind was accompanied by the rain smell of wet dust and hot asphalt, and a certain electricity in the air. Off in the distance, to the south, a low rumble of thunder shook the air.

"It's going to rain," she ventured, shouting a bit over the wind.

"Quiet," I told her, and kept her hand crushed in mine. The wind gusted through our clothes, and mixed with my anger and my fear I felt rising the electric elation that storms evoke in me. Face to the wind, hair pulled back from my scalp, I held her hand and waited: "Listen," I said, "watch, feel the storm." And after a time I felt—no, I saw, I *saw*—the sudden jerk of lightness that marked lightning. "Ah," I said aloud, counting to myself. The thunder pushed us about ten seconds later. Just a couple of miles away.

"Tell me what you see," I commanded, and heard in my own voice a vibrancy that could not be denied. Punching through the membranes . . .

"It's—it's a thunderstorm," she replied, uncertain of me in this new mood. "The clouds are very dark, and fairly low at their bottoms, but broken up in places by some largish gaps. Kind of like immense boulders rolling overhead. The lightning—there! You noticed that?"

I had jumped. "I can see lightning," I said, grinning. "I have a basic perception of light and darkness, and everything flashes to lightness for a moment. As if the sun had turned on and then off."

"Yes. It's sort of like that, only the light is shaped in jagged white lines, extending from cloud to ground. Like that model you have of subatomic particles breaking up—a sort of broken wire sculpture, white as the sun, forking the earth for just an instant, as bright as the thunder is loud." Her voice rasped with an excitement that had sparked across our hands—also with apprehension, curiosity, I didn't know what. *Light ... Blam*, the thunder struck us like a fist and she jumped. I laughed. "That was off to the side!" she said fearfully. "We're in the middle of it!"

I couldn't control a laugh. "More!" I shouted. "Pick up the pace!" And as if I were a weather-monger the lightning snapped away the darkness around us, flash-*blam* ... flash-*blam* ... flash-*BLAM!*

"We should get down!" Mary shouted over the wind's ripping, over the reverberating crashes of thunder. I shook my head back and forth and back and forth, gripped her by the arm so hard it must have hurt.

"*No!* This is *my* visual world, do you understand? This is as beautiful as it ever—" flash-*crack-blam*.

"*Carlos*—"

"No! Shut up!" Flash-flash-flash-*BOOM!* Rolling thunder, now, hollow casks the size of mountains, rolling across a concrete floor.

"I'm afraid," she said miserably, tugging away from me.

"You feel the exposure, eh?" I shouted at her, as lightning flashed and the wind tore at us, and rain drops pummeled the roof, throwing up a tarry smell to mix with the lightning's ozone. "You feel what it's like to stand helpless before a power that can kill you, is that right?"

Between thunderclaps she said, desperately, "Yes!"

"Now you know how I've felt around you people!" I shouted. *BLAM! BLAM!* "God damn it," I said, pain searing my voice as the lightning seared the air, "I can go sit in the corner park with the drug dealers and the bums and the crazies and I *know* I'll be safe, because even those people still have the idea that it isn't right to hurt a blind man. But you people!" I couldn't go on. I shoved her away from me and staggered back, remembering it all. Flash-*blam!* Flash-*blam!*

"Carlos—" Hands pulling me around.

"What."

"I didn't—"

"The hell you didn't! You came in and gave me that story about the moon, and talked backward, and drew stuff, and all to steal my work—how could you do it? How could you do it."

"I *didn't*, Carlos, I didn't!" I batted her hands away, but it was as if a dam had burst, as if only now, charged to it in the storm, was she able to speak and it all came pouring out of her, *"Listen to me!"* Flash-*blam*. *"I'm just like you.* They made me do it. They took me because I have some math background, I guess, and they ran me through more memory implants than I can even count!" Now the charged buzzing timbre of her desperate voice scraped directly across my nervous system: "You know what they can do with those drugs and implants. They can program you just like a machine. You walk through your paces and watch yourself and can't do a thing about it." *Blam.* "And they programmed me and I went in there and spouted it all off to you on cue. But you *know*"—*blam*—"was trying, you know there's the parts of the mind they can't touch—I fought them as hard as I could, don't you see?"

Flash-*blam*. Sizzle of scorched air, ozone, ringing eardrums. That one was close.

"I took TNPP-50," she said, calmer now. "That and MDMA. I just *made* myself duck into a pharmacy on my way to meet you alone, and I used a blank prescription pad I keep, and got them. I was so drugged up when we went to the Tidal Basin that I could barely walk. But it helped me to speak, helped me to fight the programming."

"You were drugged?" I said, amazed. (I know—Max Carrados would have figured it out. But me—)

"Yes!" *Boom.* "Every time I saw you after

that time. And it's worked better every time. But I've had to pretend I was still working on you, to protect us both. The last time we were up here"—*boom*—"you *know* I'm with you, Carlos, do you think I would have faked that?"

Bassoon voice, hoarse with pain. Low rumble of thunder, in the distance. Flickers in the darkness, no longer as distinct as before: my moments of vision were coming to an end. "But what do they *want?*" I cried.

"Blasingame thinks your work will solve the problems they're having getting sufficient power into a particle-beam weapon. They think they can channel energy out of the microdimensions you've been studying." *Blam.* "Or so I guess, from what I've overheard."

"Those fools." Although to an extent there might be something to the idea. I had almost guessed it, in fact. So much energy . . . "Blasingame is such a *fool*. He and his stupid Pentagon bosses—"

"*Pentagon!*" Mary exclaimed. "Carlos, these people are *not* with the Pentagon! I don't know who they are—a group from West Germany, I think. But they kidnapped me right out of my apartment, and I'm a statistician for the Defense Department! The Pentagon has nothing to do with it!"

Blam. "But Jeremy . . ." My stomach was falling.

"I don't know how he got into it. But whoever they are, they're dangerous. I've been afraid they'll kill us both. I know they've discussed killing you, I've heard them. They think you're onto them. Ever since the Tidal Basin I've been injecting myself with Fifty and MDMA, a lot of it, and telling them you don't know a thing, that you just haven't *got* the formula yet. But if they were to find out you know about them . . ."

"God I hate this spy shit!" I exclaimed bitterly. And the oh-so-clever trap in my office, warning Jeremy off . . .

It started to rain hard. I let Mary lead me down into my apartment. No time to lose, I thought. I had to get to my office and remove the trap. But I didn't want her at risk, I was suddenly frightened more for this newly revealed ally than for myself—

"Listen, Mary," I said when we were inside. Then I remembered, and whispered in her ear. "Is this room bugged?"

"No."

"For God's sake"—all those silences—she must have thought me deranged! "All right. I want to make some calls, and I'm sure my phones are bugged. I'm going to go out for a bit, but I want you to stay right here. All right?" She started to protest and I stopped her. "Please! *Stay right here,* I'll be right back. Just stay here and wait for me, *please.*"

"Okay, okay. I'll stay."

"You promise?"

"I promise."

OA. Down on the street I turned left and took off for my offices. Rain struck my face and I automatically thought to return for an umbrella, then angrily shook the thought away. Thunder still rumbled overhead from time to time, but the brilliant ("brilliant!" I say— meaning I saw a certain lightness in the midst of a certain darkness)—the brilliant flashes that had given me a momentary taste of vision were gone.

Repeatedly I cursed myself, my stupidity, my presumption. I had made axioms out of theorems (humanity's most common logical-syntactic flaw?), never pausing to consider that my whole edifice of subsequent reasoning rested on them. And now, having presumed to challenge a force I didn't understand, I was in real danger, no doubt about it; and no doubt (as corollary) Mary was as well. The more I thought of it the more frightened I became, until finally I was as scared as I should have been all along.

The rain shifted to an irregular drizzle. The air was cooled, the wind had dropped to an occasional gust. Cars hissed by over wet Twenty-first Street, humming like Mary's voice, and everywhere water sounded, squishing and splashing and dripping. I passed Twenty-first and K, where Ramon usually set up his cart; I was glad that he wouldn't be there, that I wouldn't have to walk by him in silence, perhaps ignoring his cheerful invitation to buy, or even his specific hello. I would have hated to fool him so. Yet if I had wanted to, how easy it would have been! Just walk on by, he would have had no way of knowing.

A sickening sensation of my disability swept over me, all the small frustrations and occasional hard-learned limits of my entire life balling up and washing through me in a great wave of fear and apprehension, like the flash-*boom* of the lightning and thunder, the drenching of the downpour: where was I, where was I going, how could I take even one step more?

It is important to split the great fear into component parts, because if ever they all coalesce— paralysis. I was paralyzed by fear, I felt as though I had never come down from the drugs Jeremy had given me, as though I struggled under their hallucinatory influence still. I literally had to stop walking, had to lean on my cane.

And so I heard their footsteps. Henry Cowell's *The Banshee* begins with fingernails scraping repeatedly up the high wires of an open piano; the same music played my nervous system. Behind me three or four sets of footsteps had come to a halt, just a moment after I myself had stopped.

For a while my heart hammered so hard within me that I could hear nothing else. I forced it to slow, took a deep breath. Of course

I was being followed. It made perfect sense. And ahead, at my office . . .

I started walking again. The rain picked up on a gust of wind, and silently I cursed it; it is difficult to hear well when rain is pouring down everywhere, so that one stands at the center of a universal *puh-puh-puh-puh*. But attuned now to their presence, I could hear them behind me, three or four (likely three) people walking, walking at just my pace.

Detour time. Instead of continuing down Twenty-first Street I decided to go west on Pennsylvania, and see what they did. No sound of nearby cars as I stood still; I crossed swiftly, nearly losing my cane as it struck the curb. As casually, as "accidentally" as I could, I turned and faced the street; the sonar glasses whistled up at me, and I knew people were approaching, though I could not hear their footsteps in the rain. More fervently than ever before I blessed the glasses, turned and struck off again, hurrying as much as seemed natural.

Wind and rain, the electric hum and tire hiss of a passing car. Washington late on a stormy spring night, unusually quiet and empty. Behind me the wet footsteps were audible again. I forced myself to keep a steady pace, to avoid giving away the fact that I was aware of their presence. Just a late-night stroll to the office . . .

At Twenty-second I turned south again. Ordinarily no one would have backtracked on

Pennsylvania like that, but these people followed me. Now we approached the university hospital, and there was a bit more activity, people passing to left and right, voices across the street discussing a movie, an umbrella being shaken out and folded, cars passing . . . still the footsteps were back there, farther away now, almost out of earshot.

As I approached Gelman Library my pulse picked up again, my mind raced through a network of plans, all unsatisfactory in different ways. . . . Outdoors I couldn't evade pursuit. Given. In the building—

My sonar whistled up as Gelman loomed over me, and I hurried down the steps from the sidewalk to the foyer containing the elevator to the sixth and seventh floors. I missed the door and adrenaline flooded me, then there it was just to my left. The footsteps behind me hurried down the sidewalk steps as I slipped inside and stepped left into the single elevator, punched the button for the seventh floor. The doors stood open, waiting . . . then mercifully they slid together, and I was off alone.

A curious feature of Gelman Library is that there are no stairways to the sixth and seventh floors (the offices above the library proper) that are not fire escapes, locked on the outside. To get to the offices you are forced to take the single elevator, a fact I had complained about many times before—I liked to walk. Now I was thankful, as the arrangement would give me some time. When the elevator opened at the seventh floor, I stepped out, reached back in and punched the buttons for all seven floors. Only when the door closed did it occur to me that I could have tried to find and hit the emergency-stop button, putting the elevator out of action. "Damn!" I cried. Biting my lip, I ran for my office. I started jangling through my keys for the right one, rattled by a mistake as foolish as that.

I couldn't find the key.

I slowed down. Went through them one by one. I found the key, opened my door, propped it wide with the stopper at its base. Over to the file cabinet, where I opened the middle drawer and very carefully slid one hand down the side of the correct file.

The mousetrap was gone. They knew that I knew.

AO. I don't know how long I stood there thinking; it couldn't have been long, though my thoughts spun madly through scores of plans. Then I went to my desk and got the scissors from the top drawer. I followed the power cord of the desk computer to its wall socket beside the file cabinet. I pulled out the plugs there, opened the scissors wide, fitted one point into a socket, jammed it in and twisted it hard.

Crack. The current held me cramped down for a moment—intense pain pulsed through me—I was knocked away, found myself on my knees, slumping against the file cabinets.

(For a while when I was young I fancied I was allergic to novocaine, and my dentist drilled my teeth without anesthetic. It was horribly uncomfortable, but tangent to normal pain: pain beyond pain. So it was with the shock that coursed through me. Later I asked my brother, who is an electrician, about it, and he said that the nervous system was indeed capable of feeling the sixty cycles per second of the alternating current: "When you get bit, you always feel it pumping like that, very fast but distinct." He also said that with my wet shoes I could have been killed. "The current cramps the muscles down so that you're latched on to the source, and that can kill you. You were lucky. Did you find blisters on the bottoms of your feet?" I had.)

Now I struggled up, with my left arm aching fiercely, and a loud hum in my ears. I went to my couch end table, turned on a desk lamp left there for guests, put my face to it. Light. The lights were still working, it seemed; jamming scissors into the wall socket had done nothing but destroy my hearing. Feeling panicky I ran around the corner and down to Delphina's office, remembering a day long before when the lights on the floor had gone out and I had had an opportunity to superblink around for a while, the blind leading the sightless. Somewhere behind her desk, a panel—flush with the wall, how to get it open—a wire handle, open the panel. Circuit breakers in a long vertical row. I clacked them all from left to right and ran back to my office. Face in the lamp. No sensation of light. Heat receding from the bulb. Lights out on the seventh floor.

I took a big breath. Stopped to listen. My glasses beeped fairly loudly, so I took them off and put them on a bookshelf facing the door. I tested the radio, still unsure if the floor had lost all power or not. No sound from the radio. I went into the hall briefly to look into a ceiling light. Nothing, but would I have been able to see if it were on?

Had to assume all power was gone. Back at my desk I took stapler and water tumbler, put them beside the file cabinet. I went to the bookshelves and gathered all the plastic polyhedral shapes (the sphere was just like a big cue ball), and took them to the file cabinet as well. Then I relocated the scissors on the floor.

Out in the hall the elevator doors opened.

"It's dark—"

"Shh."

Hesitant steps, into the hall.

I tiptoed to the doorway. Here it was possible to tell for sure that there were only three of them. There would be light from the elevator, I recalled suddenly, and stepped back into my room.

(Once Max Carrados was caught in a situation similar to mine, and he simply announced to his assailants that he had a gun on them, and would shoot the first person to move. In his case it had worked. But now I saw clearly that the plan was insanely risky. More verbal unreality . . .)

"Down here," one whispered. "Spread out, and be quiet."

Rustling, quiet footsteps, three small clicks (gun safeties?).

I retreated into the office, behind the side of the file cabinet. Stilled my breathing, and was silent in a way they'd never be able to achieve. If they heard anything, it would be my glasses. . . .

"It's here," the first voice whispered. "Door's open, watch it." Their breathing was quick. They were bunched up outside the door, and one said, "Hey, I've got a lighter," so I threw the pulled-open scissors overhand.

"*Ah!* Ah—" Clatter, hard bump against the hall wall, voices clashing, "What"—"threw a knife"—"*ah*"—

I threw the stapler as hard as I could, *wham*—the wall above, I guessed, and threw the dodecahedron as they leaped back. I don't know what I hit. I jumped almost to the doorway, and heard a voice whisper, "Hey." I threw the cue-ball sphere right at the voice. *Ponk.* It sounded like—like nothing else I have ever heard. (Although every once in a while some outfielder takes a beepball in the head, and it sounded something like that, wooden and hollow). The victim fell right to the hall floor, making a heavy sound like a car door closing; a metallic clatter marked his gun skidding across the floor. Then CRACK! CRACK! CRACK! another of them shot into the office. I cowered on the floor and crawled swiftly back to the file cabinet, ears ringing painfully, hearing wiped out, fear filling me like the smell of cordite leaking into the room. No way of telling what they were doing. The floor was carpet on concrete, with no vibrations to speak of. I hung my mouth open, trying to focus my hearing on the sound of my glasses. They would whistle up if people entered the room quickly, perhaps (again) more loudly than the people would be on their own. The glasses were still emitting their little beep, now heard through the pulsing wash of noise the gunshots had set off in my ears.

I hefted the water tumbler—it was a fat glass cylinder, with a heavy bottom. A rising whistle—and then, in the hall, the rasp of a lighter flint being sparked—

I threw the tumbler. *Crash*, tinkle of glass falling. A man entered the office. I picked up the pentahedron and threw it. Thump of it against the far wall. I couldn't find any of the other polyhedrons, somehow they weren't there besides the cabinet. I crouched and pulled off a shoe—

He swept my glasses aside and I threw the shoe. I think it hit him, but nothing happened.

And there I was, without a weapon, utterly vulnerable, curled over waiting to be killed, revealed in the glow of a damned cigarette lighter. . . .

When the shots came I thought they had missed, or that I was hit and couldn't feel it. Then I realized some of the shots had come from the doorway, others from the bookcase. Sounds of bodies hit, staggering, exhaling, falling, writhing—and all the while I cowered in my corner, trembling.

Then I heard a nasal groan from the hall, a groan like a viola bowed by a rasp. "Mary," I cried, and ran into the hallway to her, tripped on her. She was sitting against the wall— "Mary!" Blood on her— "Carlos," she squeaked painfully, sounding surprised.

A′. Endless moments of fear beyond fear. I had never felt anything like it. Ears ringing, hands exploring her, saying her name over and over, feeling the blood seep out of her shoulder. Feeling her harsh breath. I was bent over my stomach, sick with fear. Under my hands lay the only person I had been bold enough to love in years and years and years, and she was hurt beyond speech, barely conscious, her blood ran over my hands. If she were to die! If I were to lose her, after all that time . . .

I know, I know. That I could be so selfish in such a moment as that. The first axiom. But I barely knew her, I only knew us, I only knew what I felt. We only know what we feel.

There are eons in every hadon, when you are afraid enough. I learned that then.

Finally I gathered the courage to leave her long enough to make a call. Phones still working. 911, our number code for a scream of fear, a desperate cry for help.

And then I waited, in darkness so far beyond my daily darkness I was shocked to awareness of it. Suddenly aware that in ordinary life I walked sightless in sunlight.

And then help came.

AA′. Fortunately, it turned out that she had only been wounded. The bullet had entered just beside the shoulder, wrecking it for a long time after. But no fatal damage.

I learned this later, at the hospital. More than an hour after our arrival a doctor came out and told me, and the sickening knot of tension in my diaphragm untied all at once, making me feel sick in another way, dizzy and nauseous with relief. Unbelievably intense relief. Time lurched back to its ordinary rate of speed.

After that I went through a session with the police. Later Mary talked a lot with her employers, and we both answered a lot of questions from the FBI. (In fact, that process took days.) Two of our assailants were dead (one shot, another hit in the temple with a sphere) and the third had been stabbed: what had happened? I stayed up all through that first night explaining, retrieving and playing my tapes, and so on, and still they didn't go for Jeremy until dawn; by that time he was nowhere to be found.

Eventually I got a moment alone with Mary, about ten the following morning.

"You didn't stay at my place," I said.

"No. I thought you were headed for Blasingame's apartment, and I drove there, but it was empty. So I drove to your office and came upstairs. The elevator opened just as shots were being fired, so I hit the deck and crawled right over a gun. But then I had a hell of a time figuring out who was where. I don't know how you do it."

"Ah."

"So I broke my promise."

"I'm glad."

"Me too."

Our hands found each other and embraced, and I leaned forward until my forehead touched her shoulder (the good one), and rested.

CC′. A couple of days later I said to her, "But what were all those diagrams of Desargues's Theorem about?"

She laughed, and the rich timbre of it cut through me like a miniature of the current from my wall socket. "Well, they programmed me with all those geometrical questions for you, and I was roboting through all that, you know, and struggling underneath it all to understand what was going on, what they wanted. And later, how I could alert you. And really, Desargues's Theorem was the only geometry of my own that I could remember from school. I'm a statistician, you know, most of my training is in that and analysis. . . . So I kept drawing it to try to get your attention to *me*. I had a message in it, you see. You were the triangle in the first plane, and I was the triangle in the second plane, but we were both controlled by the point of projection—"

"But I knew that already!" I exclaimed.

"Did you? But also I marked a little *J* with my thumbnail by the point of projection, so you would know Jeremy was doing it. Did you feel that?"

"No. I xeroxed your drawings, and an impression like that wouldn't show up." So my indented copy had not included the crucial indentation. . . .

"I know, but I was hoping you would brush it or something. Stupid. Well, anyway, between us all we were making the three collinear points off to the side, which is what they were after, you see."

I laughed. "It never occurred to me," I said, and laughed again, "but I sure do like your way of thinking!"

* * *

C. I saw, however, that the diagram had a clearer symbolism than that. Points (events) determine what we are. The essential self, the disabilities, the compensations: isosceles characters projecting onto each other, distorting some features, clarifying others ... Ah yes. A fantastically complex topology, reduced to stark Euclidean triangles. Lovely.

CBA. When I told Ramon about it, he laughed too. "Here you're the mathematician and you never got it! It was too simple for you!"

"I don't know if I'd call it *too simple—*"

"And wait—wait—you say you told this here girlfriend of yours to stay behind at your house, when you knew you were going to run into those thugs at your office?"

"Well, I didn't *know* they'd be there right then. But . . ."

"Now *that* was superblink."

"Yeah."

I had to admit it; I had been stupid. I had gone too far. And it occurred to me then that in the realm of thought, of analysis and planning—in the realm where I might be most expected to deal competently with the problem—I had consistently and spectacularly failed. Whereas in the physical continuum of action, I had (up to a point) (a point that I didn't like to remember [*ponk* of sphere breaking skull, cowering revealed in a lighter's glare]) done pretty well. Though it was disturbing, in the end this reflection pleased me. For a while there, anyway, I had been almost free of the world of texts.

PQR. *Take two parallel lines*, and slide down them to their intersection, to the point at infinity. To a new haptic space:

Naturally it took a while for Mary to regain her health. The kidnapping, the behavior programming, the shooting, and most of all the repeated druggings her captors and she had subjected herself to, had left her quite sick, and she was in the hospital for some weeks. I visited every day; we talked for hours.

And naturally, it took quite a while for us to sort things out. Not only with the authorities, but with each other. What was real and permanent between us, and what was a product of the strange circumstances of our meeting—no one could say for sure which was which, there.

And maybe we never did disentangle those strands. The start of a relationship remains a part of it forever; and in our case, we had seen things in each other that we might never have otherwise, to our own great good. I know that years later, sometimes, when her hand touched mine I would feel that primal thrill of fear and exhilaration that her first touches had caused in me, and I would shiver again under the mysterious impact of the unknown other. . . . And sometimes, arm in arm, the feeling floods me that we are teamed together in an immense storm of trouble that cracks and thunders all around us, threatening every moment of our lives. So that it seems clear to me, now, that loves forged in the smithy of intense and dangerous circumstances are surely the strongest loves of all.

I leave the proof of this as an exercise for the reader.

THE RETURN FROM RAINBOW BRIDGE

When I was fifteen years old I visited the Navaho reservation north of Flagstaff, Arizona, to help the Indians celebrate the Fourth of July. Even before I arrived I thought that was kind of a strange thing to do. But something much stranger than that happened to me out there, before I left; something so strange that I have never been able to forget even the slightest detail of it, from that day to this.

On arrival late one Sunday afternoon I got out of my cousin Luke's blue VW, followed by my young brother David. My great-aunt Miriam, a tall gray-haired woman in a cotton print dress, greeted us with a sweet girlish smile, holding our hands in hers. I walked around the car to stretch my legs and survey the grounds.

As it happened our arrival coincided with the onset of a summer storm. Overhead clouds like great dark lobes of marble filled the western sky. The setting sun leaked under the edge of this front, and glazed everything with a harsh orange glare. We stood on a broad, high, bare tableland; the horizon was an immense distance away. The blacktop road merged with the dark land to east and west, one shadow ribbon among many.

Small at the center of all this space, Inscription House Mission stood before us: a church, a house, and some rough outbuildings, all whitewashed, all glowing now in the fan of stormlight, the walls' whites tinged the color of the earth, and striped with solid black shadows, but intensely bright in the surrounding gloom, like lamps at dusk. Before these suncolored walls my cousin's car, a brilliant metallic blue even in ordinary light, gleamed like the shell of a glittering scarab, a visitor from another world.

We carried our bags into my great-aunt's house just as muddy dark splotches began starring the dusty earth around us. As we entered the house I looked back, and under the gray sheets of the squall I saw a figure, standing on a bare rise to the north, near the horizon. Silhouetted, solitary, somehow more heraldic than real, it raised both arms as if to encourage the coming downpour. My first Indian, I thought, and wondered if I had seen a sort of raindance. I closed the door.

"That guy out there'll get wet," I said wisely.

"Who's that?" Luke asked, surprised.

"That Indian, out there under the storm."

He shook his head. "No one out there, far as I saw."

I opened the door again and looked out. There was nothing under the squall, no one out there on that whole broad plateau. And nowhere to hide. "What . . . ?" A gust of wind pushed at the door, as if something was trying to get in; I shivered.

That was the start of it.

While the rain drummed on the shingles of Aunt Miriam's house the four of us talked; I didn't mention again the figure I had seen. Aunt Miriam served us powdered milk. It was the first time I had drunk it, and I didn't like the taste. "It tastes funny," I said, surprised.

Aunt Miriam smiled. "It's all we've got out here."

"You get used to it," Luke said with a laugh.

The rain stopped after about half an hour, and as it was Sunday we walked over to the church to join the evening service. Yellow light from the church windows streaked the puddles in the yard, under a low black sky. The church's interior was one medium-sized room, filled with Navahos sitting in folding chairs. There were about forty of them, in rows facing a narrow lectern and a piano at the front of the room. I was surprised to see so many people; I hadn't thought very many Indians would be Christian. David and I sat in chairs set against the side wall, near the front.

An older Navaho man spoke to them in Navaho from the lectern; while he did I looked through a Bible and hymnal that had been on my chair. I saw that the Navaho language had an incredible frequency of vowels; there were words like *aanapalaooaa*, *liineaupoonaa*, *kreeaiioo* . . . it reminded me of an infant's babbling.

When the old man was done they sang hymns, Aunt Miriam accompanying them on the piano. They used the old tunes of Luther, Wesley, and Watt, but had translated the lyrics, and with all those vowels, and a wild warble in the women's voice, the familiar hymns— "A Mighty Fortress Is Our God," "Onward Christian Soldiers"—were transformed, made utterly strange, unlike any music I had ever heard. Their beauty took me by surprise, and my cheeks flushed as I listened. Up at the front Aunt Miriam sang along, an expression of pure bliss on her upraised face. She had played the flute in the Chicago Symphony, I recalled; but that could never have made her look as she did now.

While they sang these weird hymns I stared at their faces. I was a bookish youth, and I had lived all my life in a southern California suburb, a white middle-class town that couldn't have been more homogeneous if it had been legislated that way. The truth was, in my entire life I had never seen faces like these before me: dark-skinned, sun-wrinkled, hawk-nosed, heavy-lidded, life-battered faces, each the map of a world, each framed and made beautiful by sleek straight black hair, and jewelry of silver and turquoise . . . extraordinary faces: visions out of my book lore, but real. Suddenly I experienced a convulsive blush, as with the music but stronger—because I realized, right then and there, that it went beyond mere stories in books: the world was real. *The world was real.* Man, I thought, not understanding what I felt— these are really Indians!

The next morning I went outside early to walk around a bit.

The great plateau of the Navaho reservation stands over six thousand feet above sea level; I suppose that is part of the reason everything looked different to me that morning. The sky was a dark, pure blue, and in this blue the feathering of a cirrus cloud was a startling white. The cool air was hard and clear, like a glass that sharpened vision. The rainstorm had washed the land, and the earth was dark red, or the color of wet sand. Sagebrush and an occasional pine tree were scattered across the land. The sage was a shifting silvery color, like olive leaves, a shade that fit the earth tones; but the pines appeared to burst with green, as if more color had been pumped into them than they could actually hold: every pine needle poked the air, distinct in itself, dark with greenness flowing outward. I walked over to one of these pines, a juniper, I thought, feeling that I was swimming in color: red earth, green trees, blacktop road, white clouds, cobalt sky. . . .

I had been collecting the small, tight green cones of my tree for several minutes—just for something to do—when I looked up and saw that an Indian was watching me from no more than ten feet away. I jumped back, frightened; I hadn't heard him approach.

He was about my height, and somewhere in his forties or fifties, I guessed; it was hard to tell. He wore old blue jeans, a plaid cotton shirt, and a cowboy hat. His face was like those of the people in church the night before (though I hadn't seen his there): broad, impassive, masklike. "Hello!" I said nervously, afraid that I was stealing his pine cones or something.

"Hello." And he stared at me, calmly. Finally, after a long pause: "Do you like pine cones?"

"Well . . . sure! I mean they're . . . interesting!"

He looked at me. Later I became painfully familiar with that look. . . .

My nervousness increased. Finally, to break the silence, I said, "Do you live around here?"

"North some." He gestured briefly at the road. After that, silence again. He didn't seem to mind, but I was getting more uncomfortable by the second.

Perhaps he saw this. He cocked his head, watching me. "Do you play basketball?"

"Yeah!" I said, surprised. I told him about my ninth-grade team.

He nodded without expression. "Come on."

I followed him back toward the mission, confused and uncertain. Then we rounded one of the rough outbuildings, and I saw that the far end of the yard was a big basketball court. A group of Navaho men and boys were crowded under one basket, milling around in a tussle for the ball.

The man stopped beside me. "It's twenty-one. You can play if you want."

So he and I joined the game. Everyone struggled for rebounds, and when you got one the whole group was your opponent; if you managed to score anyway, you want to the free throw line and shot till you missed. Points were scored as in regular basketball, and the first person to reach twenty-one won.

It was a wild game, a free-for-all really, and I dashed around the outskirts of it somewhat at a loss. The court's surface was wet dirt sprinkled with loose gravel; not the most level of surfaces. A skinny tree trunk held up a backboard that was not quite square to the court, and the basket itself seemed unusually high, say eleven feet; perhaps it only looked that way because the backboard was so small. All in all it was not what I was used to, and when a rebound came my way I lost it dribbling. Frustrated, I got into the crowd and was elbowed and pushed with the rest of the boys as we scrambled around the men for loose balls. Impossible to hold on with six or seven hands slapping the ball; discouraged, I moved back outside, and was mostly watching when my new acquaintance took a rebound and drove into the crowd. When he was blocked off he fired a pass back over one shoulder, right at me. I got my hands up just in time to catch it, had an open moment, shot; incredibly, the ball caromed off the backboard and through the net.

At the free throw line looking up, I knew that I would miss. Even back home I couldn't make free throws, and here the basket looked twice as far away. I only hoped I would avoid an air ball.

No such luck. The ball missed everything by two feet. Involuntarily I cried out: "Aaaa!" The men and boys laughed, but in a friendly way; I had amused them by expressing aloud what everyone felt when they missed. I laughed, too, and felt more at ease. Then some men arrived and there were enough to start a real game; the boys were kicked off the court. My Indian walked over to his team without even a glance in my direction, as if he had forgotten my existence.

I sat and watched the game, and Luke joined me. "They like basketball," I said.

He cracked up. "That's right. In fact they love basketball. Basketball and pickup trucks—

those are the white man's things that the Navaho have really taken to." He laughed again. "These men—they've all got kids enough that the kids can take care of the sheep during the day. Dad can come down here and play ball with his friends, for an hour or two anyway. They play almost every day."

I pointed out my acquaintance and asked who he was.

"That's Paul. Why do you ask?"

"He brought me over here and got me in the twenty-one game."

Luke smiled. "He's a good man. He's the one I'm trying to get to hike with us to Rainbow Bridge, after the Fourth. A good man." He frowned, tossed a few pieces of gravel back onto the court. "Paul's got a son about your age. But he moved to Flagstaff."

"That's good, isn't it?" Get out there in the modern world . . .

Luke shook his head. "Alcohol's illegal on the reservation, see. It's just too much of a problem for them. So people who are . . . who want alcohol, they generally move down to Flagstaff. And then they're in trouble, because they can get it so easily."

"But he's only my age, you said!"

"That's right."

I didn't understand. He wasn't even old enough to *buy* alcohol. . . .

"Come on," Luke said, standing. "Let's go

find your brother and go for a ride. I've got to
go to the trading post."

Luke was one of those people whose internal
dynamo is pitched several thousand r.p.m.
higher than anyone else's. This was his vacation, he was just visiting Aunt Miriam (his
great-aunt too, from a different direction), but
every day he had a long list of things to do, and
he hustled around doing them until everyone
with him dropped from exhaustion. Loading
pickups with supplies, giving people rides up
dirt tracks into the back country, building
houses or fences, hunting for lost sheep: it was
all great fun to him. I would have thought that
Luke would be resented for all this help, but it
wasn't so. In fact he had a real knack for pleas-
ing the Navaho, for drawing them out. That afternoon, for instance, three times we passed
solitary Navaho men walking down the road
toward the trading post, some six miles away.
Each time Luke stopped by them, even though
after the first got in the VW was full. "Want a
ride? Where you going?" And they all got in,
so that after the third one David and I were
crushed into a corner of the backseat. The men
were forbidding in their silence, and apparently Luke didn't know any of them; it made
me nervous. But Luke laughed at the crowding,
and started asking them questions, where do
you live, how many sheep have you got, how
many kids, do you go to that VISTA place,
aren't those folks strange (they grinned), did

you get caught out in that storm yesterday . . . and by the time we got to the trading post the Navaho were talking away, both to Luke and among themselves, but always in English so we would be included, and they all took up his offer to load the VW and drive back to their homes (how are *we* going to fit in, I wanted to say), and while we were stuffing the Beetle with heavy boxes something Luke said struck them funny, I'm not sure what, and their stoic faces tilted up at the sky and broke into a million laugh lines as they cackled away. Luke just grinned, having a great time as usual. I envied him that ease, that skill.

That night at Aunt Miriam's we had mutton and bread. I had noticed the Navaho ate the same thing, every meal: bread and coffee for breakfast, mutton, bread, and coffee for lunch, and mutton, bread, and coffee for dinner. "Boy," I said, "these Navaho must sure like mutton bread and coffee!"

From the strain in my aunt's beautiful smile I knew I had said something stupid, but I didn't know what. Over the next few bites I worked it out. "They don't have anything else?"

My aunt shook her head, the smile gone.

"They have some canned stuff," Luke said. "But mutton bread and coffee, those are the staples."

I continued eating, and imagined having the meal before me, every day; it tasted different, somehow.

* * *

The Fourth of July came. In the cool morning
Paul came by in his pickup. Luke introduced
him to David and me; he nodded, smiling a little smile at me. We drove out to a gravel pit in
a dry streambed, took giant shovels and filled
the bed of the truck with gravel. Then we drove
back to the mission and shoveled the gravel
onto the basketball court.

A fresh coat for the big day. As I spread
gravel evenly over the long court I puzzled over
the idea of Indians celebrating the Fourth of
July. Shouldn't they hate this day, shouldn't
they be lighting bonfires and burning flags, or
maybe the stray white man or two?

Apparently they didn't feel that way about it.
Family after family drove up in pickup trucks.
The women set big hampers of food on the picnic tables flanking the yard. They roasted big
sides of sheep over fires set in brick pits; fra-
grant white plumes of smoke rose into the
sunny blue sky. The Navaho chatted cheerfully
with the large group of white missionaries
there for the day. The food was set out beside
paper plates, and we filed past and loaded up:
mutton, bread, and coffee—and also chili, wa-
termelon, and Cokes. A real celebration. There
must have been a hundred people there, maybe
two hundred. I wandered around eating and
watching, enjoying myself.

Only when the missionaries imposed a sequence of games on the group did the Navaho

show the slightest sign that all was not perfect on that day. As these games began they withdrew into themselves, and went along with it all impassively. A missionary friend of my aunt's called me over to him. "Come here, we need you for this one!" I was into it before I understood what the game was; when I did, I groaned. The game was this: one of the missionaries stood with his back to a group of us, and threw wrapped pieces of candy over his head in our direction, and then we scrambled to pick up as many pieces as we could.

I couldn't believe it. No wonder all the kids around me were between five and ten years old, no wonder all the Navaho boys my age had refused to join, and were now standing in the circle of observers, watching me. So *undignified* . . . Then the man threw the candy, and I gritted my teeth and went after some; damned if I could get my hands on a single piece. Those little kids were *serious* about this game, and they were fast as squirrels, and the bits of candy all disappeared almost before they hit the ground. Near the end of the ordeal I straightened up, after managing to wrestle a piece of toffee out of the clenched fist of a six-year-old, and saw the stares of all the boys my age. I felt myself flush scarlet with humiliation. And there was Paul, too, on the edge of the group, watching without expression. He said something in Navaho, and the crowd dispersed; the kids left to tally their prizes; there

was no one left for the missionary to inflict the
game on. Paul walked off, and I stared after
him gratefully, wondering what he could have
said.

Immediately I was called by the missionaries
into a volleyball game, with the boys my own
age. Ah-ha, I thought; I'll get back some lost
face, here. I had played quite a bit of volleyball
at home, and I jumped about making hits as
often as I could. Once I got an opportunity to
spike the ball over the low net, and showing off
a bit I leaped up and hit it hard. It bounced off
across the yard, a clean point for our side. Then
I saw the way all the other boys were looking
at me, faces impassive but perfectly contemp-
tuous, and I understood in a flash that they
played the game differently here; it was like
that beach paddle game, where you try to keep
the ball in play for as long as possible. Humil-
iated again, I got my brother to take my place,
and left the game. And I saw that once more
Paul had been watching, from some distance
away, standing there with his arms folded
across his chest. I gritted my teeth unhappily.

Then it was time for the basketball game, and
all the Navaho men perked up. Here was a real
game, a proper way to celebrate the holiday.

They started the game before two in the afternoon, and it didn't end till after five, and the
entire game was played in the most manic fast-
break style I had ever seen. After a shot or rebound was made, everyone broke for the other

basket, gravel spraying, the ball passed as if shot from cannons: a pass or two, a quick shot gunned, a tussle for the rebound, and off they flew the other way. Back and forth without letup, all afternoon long. I sat on the end of one bench, openmouthed at the pace of this wonderful game, and hid from the missionaries. I tried to forget the humiliations they had just caused me, but they kept coming back to mind.

Then about an hour into the game Paul jogged by and said, "Want to play?"

I jumped up and took the place of one of Paul's teammates. I was the only white man out there, and I felt keenly the eyes of the game's audience. My team seemed most comfortable ignoring me, but Paul passed me the ball once or twice, and I managed to dribble and pass it off without mishap. Once I took it and drove for the basket, then passed it out to Paul, just as he had to me in the game of twenty-one: he caught it without a hitch and pumped it through for two.

Like the rest of the men, Paul was an incorrigible gunner. He would take passes on a little rise near half-court, and fire two-handed shots straight for the sky. The ball flew two or three times as high as the basket, it seemed, then swooped down and practically ripped the net off the hoop. No fooling with the backboard for Paul. If he missed and the ball hit the rim, it made an iron crash like the hoop was breaking off, and bounced so far out or up that the rebounders were confused. But I would say he hit about sixty percent of these bombs, and many of the other men were almost as accurate. It made for a high-scoring game; although to tell the truth, I don't think they were keeping score.

I played for about twenty minutes, and left the game so beat I could hardly walk. After some rest and a couple of Cokes I recovered, and I chatted with Luke and David and Aunt Miriam while we watched the rest of the game. "These guys could beat any team in the NBA!" I said, excited. Luke grinned and added, "If it weren't for the fact that the tallest one out there is five eleven." I laughed; I was pleased; the earlier embarrassments were forgotten. The Fourth of July was turning out all right after all.

Only late that night, in bed, did it occur to me whose doing that had been.

A day or two later Luke and I drove north to Paul's home, to fix the date of our hike to Rainbow Bridge, "the biggest natural arch in the world!"—also to make sure Paul would come. Luke was a little vague about it: "Well, Paul's got a lot of responsibilities, we have to see if he's still free. . . ." Up a bumpy dirt track, rocky and pink in the surrounding tans, into the wash of a flat-bottomed canyon, past tall delicate white-barked trees, their broad green leaves translucent in the sunlight. . . .

Tucked up against the canyon wall were fences, Paul's pickup, a low oval hut. We stopped in the yard and got out. Red chickens scattered before us. There were five-gallon plastic jugs lined against one wall of the hut, which seemed *woven*, sort of: wood and wicker and perhaps *mud*, in a complex pattern. The place was quite clearly *handmade*.

Luke knocked on the wooden door and was called in: I stood in the doorway and stared into the gloom, uncertain about following. Paul was getting up from an old stuffed armchair; some others sat around a table, near a fat black stove. Paul greeted us politely, shook both our hands—because we were visiting his home, I guessed. Luke said something and they all laughed. The two men talked, and the eyes around the stove watched me. The interior walls were hung with boldly patterned rugs, earth tones cut by bright white zigzags. There were some sort of masks in the corner, it looked like. Paul and Luke were busy talking and I backed out the door, confused and uncomfortable under the gaze of Paul's family.

Penned against the little house by the fences were sheep—or goats, actually. Goats. They looked dirty, and had an awful smell. The whole place was so shabby, so small. . . . Poverty, I thought: this is what poverty looks like. Maybe I would have gone to Flagstaff too. . . .

Luke ducked out. "We're all set," he said. "He wants to take off tomorrow. Some folks on the Hopi reservation need his help in a few days, so the sooner the better for the trip."

On the drive back I had a hard time collecting myself. Luke noticed; he said, "That's a *hogan* they live in, the traditional Navaho home. You're lucky to have seen one."

I couldn't help myself: "But it was so small! And . . . dirty!"

"Not dirty. They're actually quite clean. Small, true. But it's easier to heat them that way."

"But this is the desert!" We were sweating even with the windows down.

"Yes, but in the winter it snows. Blizzards like you can't believe. Hot in the summer and cold in the winter, that's the high desert for you. It's hard to make housing that will keep you comfortable in both extremes, especially without electricity. A lot of Paul's friends are building new houses, regular framing and walls of stuccoed plasterboard. . . . They look like the houses down in Flagstaff, you probably would think they were nicer, but they freeze in the winter, and bake in the summer, and fall apart in ten years. The hogans are actually better homes."

This was interesting, and I found it comforting to an extent; but the sight of the hogan, home of the man I had thought powerful and influential—so small, dark, *primitive*—had shocked me, and that shock was more powerful than Luke's calm reasoning.

* * *

The next morning Luke woke us in the dark, and while the sky bent from indigo to the rich velvet sky blue of predawn, we drove north. David slept on the backseat, and I watched the headlight beams light the asphalt road against the dusty blond shadows of the land. Paul followed us in his truck. We drove uphill, and the low gnarled pine trees, scattered here and there like black boulders, proliferated until we drove through a kind of rocky low forest.

We parked in a gravel lot next to the Navaho Mountain Trading Post, a single wooden building, closed. The lot was empty except for us. Luke was pleased: "We'll have the whole trail to ourselves, I bet." In the morning chill we ate apples, and their cidery smell mixed with the piney odor of the trees.

Paul and Luke had packs, and David and I carried our cotton sleeping bags in rolls strapped to our shoulders. We started walking on the trail, a level white swath through the thick network of trees.

The trees shifted from black to green. The sun rose to our right, and shadows jumped down the slope to the west. Above us the east rugged sandstone ramparts alternated with steep pine-filled ravines; Navaho Mountain, Luke told us, was above and beyond the cliffs we could see. The trees were scattered everywhere now, for as far as we could see. "Piñon pines," Luke said. "Biggest stand of piñon pines in the whole world."

The broad trail was marked every mile by a metal pole, cemented in the dirt and painted bright red. Milestones, I thought. Luke laughed at them. It was fifteen miles to Rainbow Bridge.

The trail turned left, down to the west. The land began to fall away so rapidly that the trail switchbacked; here the tableland fell down into the canyons surrounding the Colorado River. We could see a long way down to the west, over tawny ridges, knobs, shadowed canyon walls. We passed milepole number five.

The trail brought us around the head of a deep canyon that snaked out to the west. "Look down there!" Luke said, pointing. "There's the trail in the canyon bottom, see it?"

There it was, far below, a white line across tan rocks. Between us and it was an immense slope like the inside of a bowl, all jumbled by stratification and erosion. "How will we get down there?" David asked.

I had been wondering that myself; I couldn't see the trail anywhere on the canyon walls. Luke started walking again, to the right rather than down. "The north side is less steep, the trail goes down there." We traversed most of a mile around the head of the canyon, then left the trees and descended the wall by following hundreds of wide switchbacks in the trail. It was fun swinging around each hairpin turn, changing directions and views as we dropped deeper and deeper into the rocky canyon world. . . .

More than an hour later we reached the canyon floor. The perspective was different down there; the broad prospect we had enjoyed up on the forested mountainside plateau was gone, and now our view was confined to the walls of the canyon we were in. Above, white-blue sky. The canyon was a deep flat-bottomed river gorge, and the trail followed the shallow pebbly stream at the bottom. Green reeds, silvery shrubs, and small cottonwoods banked this meager stream. "Cliff Canyon," Luke told us. "We'll stay in this one for a long time."

We followed the stream in its descent, milepole after milepole. I sang "Onward, Christian Soldiers" to myself as a marching song, and discovered that if I took one step for every quarter note, the hymn took me exactly one hundred steps. This seemed to me clever planning on the part of the composer. I counted steps from one red pole to the next; 1,962 steps for a mile. Four more steps and I would have hit the year. I tried to step just a little bit smaller.

We stopped and had lunch at the pool where Cliff Canyon met Redbud Pass gorge. The surface of the pool had a perfect blue sheen to it, while under it polished pebbles gleamed pink and chocolate; and the two colors, satin blue and mottled pebblestone, coexisted without mixing, both completely filling the same surface. I stared at the impossible sight, entranced.

We made the abrupt right turn and hiked up Redbud Pass gorge, and it was unexpectedly tiring to go uphill at even that slight angle. But we came to a section of the canyon that was so narrow that we had to twist to get through some parts; for almost a mile we could touch both walls at once, and they rose straight up on each side for over four hundred feet, Luke said. The sky was no more than a blue ribbon atop these endless rock walls. It was such an extraordinary thing that we were all excited: Luke sang, "Fat man's misereee!" and David and I laughed helplessly as we slipped along. We forgot we were tired, and hiked heads up until our necks hurt. Paul, bringing up the rear, had a big smile on his face: white teeth, brown skin in a million laugh lines: wild hawk face, enjoying the canyon once again, enjoying our first-time amazement.

The gorge of the pass opened up into Redbud Creek Canyon; we took a left turn and started down again. This canyon's stream made many big twists and turns, and the canyon walls S'ed with it, exposing hundreds of fluted sandstone columns, balancing boulders, smooth overhung curves, knobs like elephant heads.

I was getting a little too tired to really enjoy them, however, and poor David was beginning to drag indeed, when the canyon took a big oxbow bend to the left, and there in the outside wall of this bend was a bulge, a narrow horseshoe-shaped extension of the canyon into the cliffside. The cliff surrounding this bulge was a tall, curved, overhanging wall of rust-colored sandstone; the floor of it was flat, and just higher than the canyon floor proper. Underneath the great curving overhang was a stand of big old trees, a pool fed by a cold spring, several old picnic tables, a brick fireplace with a blackened grill on top, a stack of firewood, and scattered about, six old bedstands, stripped to metal.

"Here's camp!" Luke said, seeing our confused looks.

"But what about Rainbow Bridge?" I asked.

"It's just a little way down the canyon. Let's leave our stuff here and go have a look."

Rainbow Bridge was less than a quarter mile away; we could see it for most of the walk there. A broad arch of sandstone, it began not up atop the canyon walls as I had expected, but down at their bases, to left and right as we approached. The canyon opened up quite a bit here, so the bridge was very wide, and it rose perhaps sixty feet over us. It was flat-sided, rounded on top and bottom, streaked with brown watermarks, and sure enough, it had a broad rainbow shape to it.

Though it was no later than five or six it was gloomy down in the canyon, the sun long gone and only shining on the very tops of the walls.

The light tans and and yellows of the sandstone around us were now brown, black, blood red. I stared up at the arch. Compared to the Golden Gate Bridge, for instance, it wasn't very big. And all day I had been walking under the most fantastic contortions of sandstone that wind and water could carve ... compared to that mad sculpture, the bridge was pretty basic stuff. But it *was* unusual; and pretty big; and when you considered that it had just *happened* out here, accidental-like ... and the way it loomed in the too-bright strip of evening sky, dark as stone—a stone rainbow, the reverse of an ordinary rainbow: slab-sided, massive, permanent ...

Luke walked around it in a fever of energy, snapping pictures with his little camera. "I wish the light was better," he said. "We won't get much on film." Paul was sitting on a rock, watching him with his eyelids crinkled, amused. "This will probably be the last chance I get to photograph it in its natural state."

"What's that?" I said.

"The lake. You remember? This canyon leads down to the Colorado River, about three or four miles away. But it's Lake Powell now, you know, because of the Glen Canyon Dam. And the lake is still rising. This canyon is flooding, and they say you'll be able to boat right under the bridge in a couple of years."

"You're kidding!"

"Nope. This'll be water, right here where we

stand. It might even flood the whole bridge, although they say it won't." Luke was matter-of-fact about it; that was just the way it was, nothing to get upset over, not when there was nothing to be done.

I glanced over at Paul. No expression on his face, none at all. The Navaho mask . . . he was looking up at the streaked sides of the arch. I walked under it again, on solid ground, and stared up at it. Massive rust band against the sky . . . it looked different, somehow.

That evening, as night fell and the stars appeared in the arc of sky standing over the cliffs, we started a fire in the brick fireplace and cooked hot dogs for dinner. The flames cast a warm, flickering yellow on the overhanging back wall. This smooth sweeping curve echoed our voices, and the crackling wood, and the low gurgle of the water leaving the spring's pool; it amplified the *whoo* of the wind flowing down-canyon.

We devoured the hot dogs, ate three or four apiece. Afterwards I walked around the camp a little. The big old trees had crumpled gray-green bark, gnarled branches, leaves as smooth and prickly-edged as holly leaves. The bare metal bedsteads gave the place the look of a ruin: giant cathedral, roof fallen in, trees growing up out of the floor, altar a fireplace, beds dragged in. . . . The wind hooted and the sharp-edged leaves clattered, and feeling spooked I returned to the others.

After we had laid out our sleeping bags and gotten into them, I still felt . . . strange. I had chosen to sleep on one of the picnic tables, and was under one of the trees. Between the black leaves the stars appeared and disappeared, pricking at my sight, creating a sense of constant movement that was not necessarily in the leaves. There were a lot of little noises, echoing off the overhang. I had seldom if ever slept outdoors before, and it felt . . . exposed, somehow. Someone could just sneak right up on you! They could sneak up and murder all of us down here, and no one would know! Well, that was silly. But stuck so deep in this deep canyon, with the vault of the sky so far above the tree-filled black horseshoe bend, and the wind whistling over the rock, the world seemed a vast place: vast, dark, windy. . . . I lay there for a long time before falling asleep.

I woke in the middle of the night, having to pee. Something in me resisted getting up: fear of the open darkness, clutching at me. But I had to go and I slid out of my sleeping bag and stepped off the picnic bench, walked down toward the bridge, out of the camp.

Once out from under the trees a great map of stars sheltered me. In their brilliance I recognized not a single constellation. It seemed the moon might be rising, or else the starlight was brighter here than I was used to; the canyon walls caught enough illumination to reveal some of their hieroglyphics of erosion. It was chill but not cold; I walked down the trail to take a brief look at the bridge in this strange light.

A man stood directly beneath the bridge, both arms raised to the sky. Paul ... I recognized the gesture as that made by the solitary figure I had seen greeting the storm on the evening we had arrived—the figured that had disappeared!—and I understood that that had been Paul out there. He was some sort of ... I didn't know what.

He turned around, aware of being watched, and saw me. Reluctantly I walked down the trail and joined him.

"You're up late," I said.

"So are you."

We stood there. As my eyes adjusted further to the dark—as the moon, perhaps, rose further in the blocked-off sky to the east—I could see his face better: crags of weathered flesh, shadowed fissures deeply scored; it looked like the sandstone around us. Water sounds, small but distinct, played between us; wind sounds, soft but large, soughed over us, as if the canyon were an immense flute that someone was breathing through. ... By moving my head a little I could make stars wink in and out of existence, there at the black edges of the arch.

"How can they flood this place?" I said quietly.

Paul shrugged. "Build a dam . . ."

"Oh, I know. I know. But . . . can't you stop it?"

He shook his head.

"I wish you could. . . ."

"It doesn't matter." I was about to protest that it did, when he raised a hand and held it out between us. A narrow silver ring blinked starlight, there on his little finger. "The bridge is like the ring. Your people come to see it, on foot like you have, and soon by boat. Many people. But while the ring takes the attention like that, the rest of the hand—the rest of the body—it's all left alone."

"You mean the reservation."

"All the land here, all the canyons. This ring is precious, but it isn't the body. There are hundreds of canyons out here—canyons and mesas, mountains, rivers without an end to them. Arches, yes. To have all the attention on this bridge, all the visitors . . . it's not such a bad thing."

"I see. I understand."

"Places only we know about are let be . . . cliff dwellings."

"Like the Inscription House ruin?" I said.

"Yes, like that. Only hidden. Never found, you see. Lost forever, perhaps. Let be forever."

Then we were silent, listening to the great flute channel the wind. I thought of Rainbow

Bridge as a giant stone ring, buried just a bit more than halfway into the earth. The light in the canyon grew ever stronger, though the sky to the east remained a pure black, the stars there wavering intensely in the shiver of the atmosphere.

"Do you think your son will ever come back?" I said.

He glanced at me, surprised. The wet surface of his eyes reflected tiny pinpoint stars. ". . . Yes," he said finally. "But when he does"—tapping his head with a finger—"a part of him will be dead."

My head felt as if he had tapped me, just over the ear. Quickened—

I woke from the dream with a start. It was dark, stars blinked in the black mesh of branches over me. The stiff, sharp-edged leaves clicked against each other. The dream hesitated on the leaf edge of oblivion—slipped back into my memory, intact. I thought about it.

I did have to pee. I got out of the sleeping bag, stepped off the picnic table, walked around the tree.

When I was done I rounded the tree and almost ran into him. "Ah!" I leaped back, tripped, almost fell.

"Hey," Paul said softly, helping me get to my feet. "It's just me." He let go of me, looked at me. In the dark I couldn't read his expression;

I could barely see it. "Still me." He walked past me, toward his bedroll.

When I got back in my sleeping bag my heart was still thumping, as loud in my ears as snapped fingers. *Still me* . . . The side of my head tingled. I looked up at the patternless smeary white stars, sure it would take me hours to fall asleep again; but I don't recall staying awake for even so much as a minute.

The next morning we ate a breakfast of crackers and oranges, rolled our bags and packed our gear, poured water on the ashes of the fire, and took off. It was a warm morning, the cliff-rimmed patch of sky a clear pale blue. Paul didn't mention our encounter of the previous night; in fact he said hardly a word during breakfast, and led the way up the canyon without looking back. Luke, David and I followed.

It didn't take long to discover that hiking back up out of the canyons was harder than descending into them. Yesterday I hadn't even noticed how continuous the descent was; now every step up spoke to me. And at some 1,962 steps per mile . . . for fifteen miles . . . I couldn't finish the multiplication in my head, but I knew it was a lot of walking.

We had a short respite, going down the Redbud Pass gorge, and the narrow section was still wonderful; but once in Cliff Canyon it was uphill for good. The sun burst over the south wall of the canyon, and the day got hot. Frequently we stopped to drink. We stayed in the same order: Paul, me, David, Luke. I started to sing "Onward, Christian Soldiers," but looking at Paul's back before me I felt stupid doing it, and I stopped.

David was the first to give out; he sat down by a pool and rolled onto his back. I was kind of proud of him: he had walked until he dropped, without a single word of complaint. A tough kid, my little brother.

We sat by the pool and considered it. David, nearly asleep where he lay, was clearly played out. Luke, unworried and cheerful, filled David's water cup at the pool. "Why don't you two go on ahead," he said to Paul and me. "You can take Paul's truck back to the mission, and that way Aunt Miriam won't worry about us. I'll come up with David either late tonight, or tomorrow morning."

Paul and I nodded, and after a short rest the two of us started off.

After about an hour of hiking behind Paul, watching Cliff Canyon broaden and open up, I saw the canyon's head. Before us stood a curved slope just as steep as the walls to right and left. This was where the trail had that long sequence of switchbacks, ascending the left wall, reaching the tableland above, and then skirting the canyon's rim up there, to a patch of piñon over on the top of the right wall. I could even see where the trail went, up among those tiny trees; it was so *far* above. I couldn't believe how far above it was; surely we hadn't come down from there!

Later I learned that the trailhead is three thousand feet higher than Rainbow Bridge; and a full fifteen hundred of those vertical feet are climbed right there, on the headwall of Cliff Canyon. At the time, it looked even taller than that. And the worst part of it, as far as I was concerned, was that the trail took such a gigantic detour to the left! It effectively doubled the distance we had to go to reach that patch of piñon pine on the top of the right wall. And all those dumb switchbacks, adding distance too. . . . I couldn't believe it.

I was tired, I wanted an easier way. "Listen," I said to Paul, "couldn't we just head straight up the right slope to where the trail goes through those trees? It isn't much steeper than the trail side, and we'd get it over with that much faster."

Paul shook his head. "The trail's the best way."

But I had convinced myself, and stubbornly I argued to convince him. "You can see the whole slope from here to there—just dirt—no brush to walk through—nothing to it! It's just like a stairway all the way up! And then we wouldn't have to go way off the wrong way!" On and on I went.

Paul watched me without expression. No

agreement with my points; no irritation that I would debate the best route with him; just an impassive gaze, staring at me. That look, becoming familiar: did it hide a laugh?

Finally, after I had repeated my points many times, he looked away, off into the distance. "You go that way, then. I'll take the trail, and meet you up in those trees."

"All right," I said, happy to have my way. I thought it was an excellent plan. "I'll see you up there."

He turned and trudged up the dusty white trail.

It's hard for me now to believe that I could have been that stupid. To think a cross-country route would be easier than trail; to argue with a Navaho about the best way to get from one point to another, in Navaho country; to ignore Paul's judgment, and go off on my own . . . incredible. But I was fifteen, and I was tired, and I wanted an easier way. I wished one into existence, and took off.

I started up the slope. The footing was good, and I made good progress. I imagined greeting Paul at the top when he finally appeared by way of the trail. I glanced over at the other side of the canyon to see how far he had gotten, but the trail followed a crease that was probably the streambed when it rained enough, and there was a bulge in the wall between my slope and that crease, so he was out of sight. I could still see the trees at the top, however; and after a short rest I pressed on.

The canyonside I ascended was sandstone. No doubt it had been formed as successive layers of some primordial beach, eons ago; in any case it was horizontally stratified, and this meant I climbed something very like an ancient staircase, weathered now almost out of existence. Stone ledges protruded from the angled slope of grainy dirt, giving me a few inches of flat surface to step up on. On the dirt itself it was harder; the angle stretched my Achilles tendons, and there was a slight tendency to slip back that had to be resisted.

It was hot, and there was no wind. The sun blazed overhead so that a big quadrant of sky was too white to look at. I had to wipe sweat from my eyebrows to keep it from getting in my eyes and stinging. Once the dirt beneath my shoe gave way, and I went down to one knee, and got up with my sweaty hands all dirty.

Time passed. I began to zigzag a little to decrease the angle of the slope, and give my Achilles tendons a break. I was still low in the canyon. Looking up, I could no longer see all the way to the top; steep points in the slope along the way intervened, and became my temporary skyline. Luckily, the configuration of the slope itself kept me on course: I was climbing a sort of rounded ridge, and if I deviated too far to left or right, the angle of the slope became quite a bit steeper. So I was following the edge of an indistinct buttress (though I didn't know that), and thus I had a clear route.

Onward and upward. I began taking a rest every hundred steps. I had already come to the conclusion that the trail would have been easier: you could step flat on the trail, and you didn't slide backward half the time, and you didn't have to figure out which way to go every step of the way. I felt foolish, as one always does at the halfway station between innocence and experience. Blake missed that category: *Songs of Foolishness.*

The terracing of sandstone ledges began to get more distinct, and larger in scale. Instead of stairs, they were waist or chest high, as if they were stairs for giants, with vertical sections to them that were steeper than I was used to. So each ledge had to be climbed, or else I had to zigzag a route up the various dry gullies that broke through these ledges. It was hard work. Looking up I could usually only see a hundred feet or so at a time, and the view never changed; it kept on like that no matter how long I went between rests. The day got hotter.

I had no hat. I had no water. I had no food. I had no map, or compass (though they wouldn't have done me any good if I had had them). In fact, I had nothing but a cotton sleeping bag hanging from my shoulders, and its straps were really cutting into my arms. I couldn't see my destination anymore, but judging by the canyon below, and the great wall across from me, I still had a long, long way to go. And the way kept getting harder.

Slowly but surely, fear began to seep into me. What if I lost my way, and somehow missed the exact knot of piñon pines that marked where the trail was? It would be impossible to find the trail without that landmark. And then what if I couldn't go on without water, and couldn't find any? Or—I slipped hard and banged my knee on a ledge, which made me cry out with fear—what if I hurt myself so badly I couldn't walk? This slope was so immense, no one would ever find me on it.

I shoved these fears away and climbed on a bit faster, spurred by their presence, pushing in around the edges of conscious thought. But soon enough the surge of adrenaline they had caused was used up, by a hard scramble up a dry streambed. As I got more and more tired it became impossible to hold the fears out of my thoughts, and they came pouring back in. My head ached, in a tight band across the temples. My tongue was a thick, dry thing clogging my mouth; it tasted of dust, and I couldn't work up a bit of saliva. My breaths were like ragged sobs.

The sun had shifted far to the west, and the rocks threw shadows off to the left. The light had that ominous, dark brilliance that sometimes comes late in the day after a cloudless noon, with the lengthening shadows and a mare's tail or two of cloud in the sky. Above me the slope appeared to steepen, into a genuine staircase shape of horizontal, vertical, horizontal, but on a giant's scale, the little cliffs of the verticals now ten feet tall.

The time came when panic overwhelmed me. Not in a single rush, but in a growing crescendo of fear, that pushed, and pushed, and finally became *panic*, that flood of fear-beyond-fear, fear pushed up into another plane . . . how to describe it? All my senses were heightened, though their input seemed malignant: I could feel tiny puffs of breeze chilling my sweat-soaked back, could see every individual pebble and sand grain, for as far as the canyons extended . . . I could feel my breathing, all my muscles, my blood washing about in me, pumping hard through the heart. I knew that I could die, astonishing knowledge for a fifteen-year-old. But I also knew that I still lived, and could act. Panic-stricken, in a sort of exuberance of fear, I climbed again, ignoring the complaints of my muscles and the niceties of the best route, scrambling hard where I had to, moving resolutely upward, attacking the obstacles furiously . . . I suppose I had never been quite as alive as in those moments, ever in my life.

In fact I suppose that all my subsequent interest in the extremities of physical endurance, in the exploration of the bleak and harsh parts of the globe—the poles, the high mountains, the deserts—was born in those moments, when I felt the reality of such extremity myself. Ever afterwards I would know what it felt like to be pressed to the edge, I would remember the strange surge into that other world of panic spring . . . and the memory of it creates a certain (is it morbid?) fascination. . . .

Unfortunately, purest panic cannot last very long, and when it washed out of me, step by weary step, I pressed on in dull misery. As I forced myself up I wondered what Paul would think when I died and never showed up.

His face, hawklike under the gleaming black hair, popped into sight over a ledge above me. "Paul!" I cried. "Here!"

He saw me and grinned. "Glad to see you!"

"*You're* glad to see *me!* Wow—" I laughed tearfully. "I was hoping you'd look for me. I've been sort of lost down here. . . ."

"There's still a way to go. Here, come up this way, up this crack."

I followed his directions, almost giggling with relief. "Oh, man," I said, remembering the last hour. "Oh, man!" I reached the ledge he was on and stood next to him. We looked at each other. Maybe this time there was the slightest expression on his face: a raised pair of eyebrows. Well, boy?

I shrugged sheepishly, looked down: "How long did you wait for me?"

"An hour or so."

"It—it was harder than it looked."

"That's almost always true, around here. Get

far enough away and you can't see ledges like this at all—they just look water streaks."

"That's right! Why from below it looked like a smooth walk all the way."

He didn't reply. We stood there. "I think I can go on now," I said.

He nodded. We started climbing the slope; I followed him, put my feet in his footprints, which saved me some sliding. Up and up, step after step. He stopped often so we could rest.

I was lucky he had come down to look for me, because the slope of the wall, like the inside of a bowl, got steeper as we approached the top. The vertical sections were now sometimes twelve or fifteen feet tall, while the flat ledges narrowed to little sitting platforms. . . . Time after time Paul found breaks in these faces, footholds, dry streambeds, routes of one sort or another, so that using hands to pull ourselves, we could make our way up.

"Man, how did you get *down* here?" I asked during one rest.

"Same way we're going up—that's how I know the way. It's a lot easier seeing the way down. Harder to actually do it, but if you're patient it's not bad."

On and up. We came to one cliff about fifteen or eighteen feet high—trouble. The only way up that didn't force a long detour was a sequence of knobs and notches that had to be climbed like a ladder. Paul climbed it and showed me the holds. I took a deep breath and started up after him; his head poked over the top as he watched me.

I was almost to him when my right foot slipped out of its niche. The other foot went too, and I was falling when he grabbed me by the wrist. One hand, clamped on my wrist, holding me up; I couldn't get a purchase on the sandstone I was knocking against. My hand caught his wrist, so we were twice linked.

"Be still." I looked up; his neck muscles bulged out, his mouth was pursed. "I pull you up to here, you grab the ledge with your other hand. Then get a knee over. Ready?"

"Yeah," I gasped. I felt his hand crush my wrist as he prepared for the pull, and then I was scraped up the sandstone, and scrabbling for a handhold on the ledge, pulling up, left knee up and over, like high jumping—and I was on the ledge, face in the gritty dirt. Paul was sprawled back on the ground, still holding on to my wrist. He sat up, smiling a small smile.

"You okay?"

I nodded breathlessly, looking at the white finger marks on my wrist. I didn't want to start crying, so I didn't say anything.

"We'll find a better way up any others like that. Come on."

I staggered up and followed him. True to his word, we were able to climb gulleys to make it up every vertical slab. I was thankful; by this point I was past any extra efforts. It was hard just to walk.

Then the slope tilted back, got easier. We snaked up a little gully that was like a miniature of the canyons below. And we came out of the top of it into trees—piñon pines, on flat sandy ground. The top. And there, just by the first trees, threading its way among them, was the trail, a wide whitish trough.

"Oh, good," I said.

Paul stopped in the trail and we rested. He saw the look on my face and said, "Cross-country can be hard."

I nodded mutely.

"The hard way can teach you a thing or two, though. Here. You lead. Set whatever pace you're comfortable with. We still have a way to go."

It was true, but I didn't care. We were on the trail. I walked along it zombielike. It was amazing how easy it was to walk on a trail; no decisions to make at all, no terrible stretch of foot and Achilles tendon . . . wonderful thing, trail. How long had I been off it? Four hours, five? It seemed much longer than that, but the sun still shone, there was a good deal of daylight left; it couldn't have been more than five hours. What a lot of living to fit into such a small span! What a lot of appreciation for trail, to have gained in only five hours!

I was hiking along the trail through the pines, and half thinking thoughts such as these, when I rounded a corner and saw Paul lying there ahead of me, sacked out asleep under a tree, his cowboy hat shading his face.

I jerked to a stop, spun around. No Paul following me on the trail. I had heard his steps behind me just a moment before.

I turned again, confused. The Paul under the tree heard me, tipped up his cowboy hat, saw me. He sat up, calm and slow. "You made it," he said.

I felt the skin on my back crawl. I began to tremble, and for a second light-headedness washed through me, almost made me sick. My vision returned with scores of crawling clear tubes in it. "How—how long have you been here?"

He shrugged. "An hour or so. You get lost?"

I shook my head. "You didn't . . ." I couldn't finish.

He stood, put on his pack, came over and looked at me. He cocked his head curiously . . . something in his look, there . . . not complicity, but perhaps an acknowledgment that I had a right to be confused. . . .

"Here," he said. "Want me to take that sleeping bag?"

"You won't m—you won't mind?" Because my shoulders were aching fiercely under the straps.

He smiled a little—just exactly the smile he had had on his face after he pulled me up the cliff. My wrist tingled with the memory of that crushing grip, and when he touched my arm to slip the sleeping bag off, I almost cried out. I sat down right on the spot, trembling all over, my skin rippling in great shivers of nervous shock, of fear. Rippling fields of goose bumps . . . "But I . . ." But I was too frightened of him to be able to ask him anything. I looked back the way I had come, thinking he might still appear; yet here he was before me, taking off his pack, tying my sleeping bag to the top of it. . . .

He got it secured, put the pack back on. He looked at me, concerned. "It's okay."

I wiped the tears from my face. Nodded, looking down, ashamed. It was emphatically not okay. But there was nothing for it but to stand, to follow him down the trail.

He stepped in front of me, caught my ashamed gaze, reached out and touched my arm with a single finger. "It's okay, now." Something in his voice, his eyes—as if he knew everything that had happened. . . .

My shivering stopped, I nodded meekly. "Okay. Let's go."

But all the way back I thought of it. The trailhead was a long way across the tableland, and it was a miserable hike, through the long shadows of the last part of the day, sky already darkening with the sun still up, lenticular cloud over Navaho Mountain glowing the color of the canyons, every little wave of it a perfectly drawn French curve. . . . Cruelly, the Park Service had set the red milepoles farther and farther apart the closer to the trailhead you came; I hadn't noticed on the way in. I tried counting steps one to the next and lost count in the first hundred.

Maybe he had gone down to get me, then as we hiked up the trail, had snuck ahead through the trees to lie down and give me a surprise. Only he couldn't have: the trail cut through a sort of notch there, with thick forest on each side. From the time I last saw the Paul behind me until the first moment I saw the Paul under the tree, only a couple of minutes had elapsed. There just wasn't time for such a maneuver. No ... I began to shiver again. Each time I forced myself to truly confront the memory of what had happened, I was racked with electric shivers running up and down my back, then all over me, and the spasm shook my head violently, as if my spine were a branch and my head a fruit, orange or apple or pear, that someone was trying to bring down. . . .

In a garish desert sunset we reached the trading post, the parking lot. The trading post was open, and we went in. While Paul spoke in Navaho I went to the big cooler in the corner, one of those refrigerated metal trunks that stands waist high. I flipped the top hatch open and pulled out a Nehi Grape drink; pulled off the flip top and drank it down in two long swallows. I can still remember perfectly the strange carbonated grape flavor of that drink. When I was done I got out another can and drank it too.

Paul drove us home through the dusk, his pickup's big headlight beams bouncing about in tandem as we hit potholes in the asphalt. I was too tired to think much, but once the sight of Paul lying there under that tree, hat over his face, flashed before me, and the goose bumps rippled over me again, like the wind shooting cat's paws over the surface of a lake. My whole nervous system resonated with fear, I once again felt his hand clamped on my wrist, my knees scraping the sandstone, feet free in the air, searching for purchase. . . . I've never had a better demonstration of how completely our skins are linked to our minds. Then the fit passed, and I slumped in the seat again, sweating, watching the headlight beams lance the darkness.

Maybe I had gone crazy. Yeah, that was it: I had gone crazy and hallucinated Paul's presence with me on that canyonside. And I must have hallucinated that fall, too, because if I really had fallen it was certain no hallucination was going to catch me and pull me up. Sure. The whole thing, just a frightened sunstruck dream.

The only trouble was, I knew that it hadn't been. Oh, I know, you can say if you went crazy then you were crazy, and you couldn't tell what was real and what wasn't. But that isn't the way it works, not in the real world. I mean, that's the sad thing about insane people; almost all of them know perfectly well that something is seriously wrong with them; that's what makes them so scared, so depressed. They know.

And I knew, I *knew*, that I had not hallucinated that slip and fall, or the hand on my wrist. It was all a seamless whole, from the start up the slope to the finish in the trees, and no anxious half hour—not even a half hour of panic—could have made me so crazy that my senses could have been fooled that badly. Later, when the memory faded some, I could doubt that point; but there in the truck with Paul, my wrist still aching, the whole memory of it still in my body, I was certain of it.

Finally we were back at the mission. Aunt Miriam came out to greet us, and we told her about Luke and David. Paul said he'd go back up the next day to make sure they got out all right; he glanced at me as he said it. And he smiled as he said good night, that small smile I had seen before. . . . For a second I saw in his eyes a clear acknowledgment of what had happened. And I understood: Paul was an Indian sorcerer, he could be in two places at once. But then he was gone, and I wasn't so sure.

I found that my skin could ripple with goose bumps even immersed in the hot water of my aunt's old bathtub; all I had to do was remember that look, that smile, the moment on the cliff face, seeing Paul under that piñon. . . . Despite my exhaustion, I slept very poorly that night; I kept jerking awake as I slipped off the face . . . and it would all come pouring in again, until I moaned at the bright fresh fear of it. Would it never ease, this fear?

The next day about noon Luke and David drove up in Luke's VW, laughing over great adventures of their own: Luke had carried David part of the way, they had slept in the trail, Luke had hiked to the trading post and back in the middle of the night, to make sure no one was waiting and worrying. . . . These adventures sounded quite mundane to me. Luke had already heard some of what had happened to me from Paul, and he laughed at my silence, thinking I was only embarrassed at ignoring Paul's advice and taking off cross-country. I imagine I didn't show much of a sense of humor about it.

The day after that it was time to leave. Luke was going to drive us all the way to Phoenix to catch a plane, and then come all the way back; he was looking forward to the drive.

We were out front saying our good-byes to Aunt Miriam when Paul drove up in his truck. Only later did it occur to me that he had come specifically to say good-bye to us. To me. Only later did I recall we were driving through Flagstaff, only later did I put it together, that for Paul I was . . . I don't know what, exactly.

He got out, walked over. Same jeans, same

shirt . . . He smiled at David and me, shook our hands. I recognized the grip, recognized it exactly. He looked me in the eye, nodded once, solemnly, as if to confirm my thought: *it happened.* He tapped the side of his head with his finger. "That was a good hike," he said to me. "Remember."

We got into the VW. As we drove off, Paul and Miriam stood side by side, waving—Paul looking right at me, nowhere else—and the two of them had identical expressions on their faces, that expression you see in the faces of your older relatives, as you wave good-bye to them after an infrequent, too-short visit; they're fond of you, they love you, they look at you with an honesty only the old have, thinking this might be the last good-bye, the last time they will ever get to see you: *pleasure; sorrow; will I see that one again before I die?*

Remember. Many years have passed since that happened; my great-aunt Miriam died in 1973, and as it turned out I never did see her again. And I never heard another word of my friend Paul, from that time to this.

But I've thought about him, oh believe me I have: and every single time I have brought myself to think honestly about it, to remember it truly and admit to myself that such an impossible thing happened to me, my skin has reacted with its fearful shivered rippling; just a ghost of the original fear in its power to shake me, but still most definitely there, a cold, uncanny contacɪ with ... something *other*. Even writing this account, here in a quiet room halfway around the world, nineteen years away, I have felt that shiver—once, in fact, as strongly as any since the first time: the room disappeared, and I was back there in those pines, Paul lying there ...

Naturally I have attempted, many times, to explain to myself what happened that afternoon. I have read of the Indian shamans of the Southwest with more than the usual interest, and recalling the masks and jugs I glimpsed so briefly at Paul's hogan, I suspect he could have been one. The Navaho are a pretty secular people, but Paul had business with the Hopi, unusual for a Navaho; and you don't get any stranger than the Hopi. And the Navaho treated Paul differently, too, he had a sort of power over them.... People are skeptical of Castañeda, and I suppose they should be—I probably would be too—but sometimes when I was reading those books, that shaman spoke right to me, through a face I knew.... Yes, it could be I was befriended by a shaman, and shown a little of the world beyond.

And of course the idea has returned to me, often, that I hallucinated Paul's presence, in my fear and need calling up his image to get me up the last, most difficult part of the climb. Sure. It's the explanation that makes the most sense, the one I believe in myself most often.

But . . . a hallucinated figure, an imagined conversation, those are one thing; a hallucinated cliff face, an imagined fall? For me, somehow, those are in a different category; and I have never been able to believe that I was that completely disconnected from reality. Because that *hand on my wrist!* My God, how to tell it? I was hanging there in space, falling, and that hand on my wrist *pulled me up.* It pulled me up to safety, to the life I have lived since then. . . . And I *felt it.*

So. In the end, I always have to let it be. Something strange happened to me, out there in the desert; I don't know what.

But lately, when I think about it, I always see the look that was on Paul's face as we drove away from the mission, and out of his life. And I see him trying to jump the giant gap between our lives, to teach me a little, mostly with looks; I see him letting me hike off on my own; I feel that hand on my wrist, pulling me up. . . . And now when I remember that impossible moment, I have been filled with some sort of huge, cloudy feeling—call it grace: my spirit has soared at the thought of it, flying like a shaman over the surface of this world, exhilarated and intensely happy. Either way it was a gift, you see; a gift from Paul, or from the world. Because consider it: if Paul was a shaman, and out of his feeling for me sent his spirit down that canyon wall to help me up, while the rest of him slumbered there in the sun under a piñon pine—then human beings have mysterious powers that we poor civilized rational people are unaware of, and we are much greater than we know. But if, on the other hand, I imagined Paul's presence there above me, if only I was there to clasp myself as I fell, so that I pulled myself up that cliff, by the power of my mind, and by the strength of my desire to live—then we are free indeed.

I have a battery radio—there are so many work stoppages because of the power failures, and days the water has to be boiled, and so on, that you really have to have a radio to save wasting time and dying of typhoid—and Simon turned it on while I was making supper on the Primus. The six o'clock All-American Broadcasting Company news announcer announced that peace was at hand in Uruguay, the president's confidential aide having been seen to smile at a passing blonde as he left the 613th day of the secret negotiations in a villa outside Katmandu. The police action in Arizona was going well; the Neo-Birch insurgents in Phoenix could not hold out much longer against the massed might of the American army and air force, since their underground supply of small tactical nukes had been cut off. Then there was an advertisement for Fed-Cred cards, and a commercial for the Supreme Court: "Take your legal troubles to the Nine Wise Men!" Then there was something about why tariffs had gone up, and a commercial for U.S. Government canned water, with a catchy little tune: "Don't be sorry when you drink / It's not as healthy as you think / Don't you think you really ought to / Drink coo-ool, puu-uure U.S.G. water?"—with three sopranos in close harmony on the last line. Then, just as the battery began to give out and his voice was dying away into a faraway tiny whisper, the announcer seemed to be saying something about a new continent emerging.

"What was that?"

"I didn't hear," Simon said, lying with his eyes shut and his face pale and sweaty.

The Tor SF Doubles

Ursula K. Le Guin

THE NEW ATLANTIS

A TOM DOHERTY ASSOCIATES BOOK
NEW YORK

THE NEW ATLANTIS

A TOR Book
Published by Tom Doherty Associates, Inc.
49 West 24 Street
New York, NY 10010

Cover art copyright © 1989 by Michael Böhme. Used by permission of the Luserke Agency.

ISBN: 0-812-50010-5   Can. ISBN: 0-812-50114-4

First edition: October 1989

Printed in the United States of America

0 9 8 7 6 5 4 3 2 1

Coming back from my Wilderness Week I sat by an odd sort of man in the bus. For a long time we didn't talk; I was mending stockings and he was reading. Then the bus broke down a few miles outside Gresham. Boiler trouble, the way it generally is when the driver insists on trying to go over thirty. It was a Supersonic Superscenic Deluxe Longdistance coal-burner, with Home Comfort, that means a toilet, and the seats were pretty comfortable, at least those that hadn't yet worked loose from their bolts, so everybody waited inside the bus; besides, it was raining. We began talking, the way people do when there's a breakdown and a wait. He held up his pamphlet and tapped it— he was a dry-looking man with a schoolteacherish way of using his hands—and said, "This is interesting. I've been reading that a new continent is rising from the depths of the sea."

The blue stockings were hopeless. You have to have something besides holes to darn onto. "Which sea?"

"They're not sure yet. Most specialists think the Atlantic. But there's evidence it may be happening in the Pacific, too."

"Won't the oceans get a little crowded?" I said, not taking it seriously. I was a bit snappish, because of the breakdown and because those blue stockings had been good warm ones.

He tapped the pamphlet again and shook his head, quite serious. "No," he said. "The old continents are sinking, to make room for the new. You can see that that is happening."

You certainly can. Manhattan Island is now under eleven feet of water at low tide, and there are oyster beds in Ghirardelli Square.

"I thought that was because the oceans are rising from polar melt."

He shook his head again. "That is a factor. Due to the greenhouse effect of pollution, indeed Antarctica may become inhabitable. But climatic factors will not explain the emergence of the new—or, possibly, very old—continents in the Atlantic and Pacific." He went on explaining about continental drift, but I liked the idea of inhabiting Antarctica and daydreamed about it for a while. I thought of it as very empty, very quiet, all white and blue, with a faint golden glow northward from the unrising sun behind the long peak of Mount Erebus. There were a few people there; they were very quiet, too, and wore white tie and tails. Some of them carried oboes and violas. Southward

the white land went up in a long silence toward the Pole.

Just the opposite, in fact, of the Mount Hood Wilderness Area. It had been a tiresome vacation. The other women in the dormitory were all right, but it was macaroni for breakfast, and there were so many organized sports. I had looked forward to the hike up to the National Forest Preserve, the largest forest left in the United States, but the trees didn't look at all the way they do in the postcards and brochures and Federal Beautification Bureau advertisements. They were spindly, and they all had little signs on saying which union they had been planted by. There were actually a lot more green picnic tables and cement Men's and Women's than there were trees. There was an electrified fence all around the forest to keep out unauthorized persons. The forest ranger talked about mountain jays, "bold little robbers," he said, "who will come and snatch the sandwich from your very hand," but I didn't see any. Perhaps because that was the weekly Watch Those Surplus Calories! Day for all the women, and so we didn't have any sandwiches. If I'd seen a mountain jay I might have snatched the sandwich from his very hand, who knows. Anyhow it was an exhausting week, and I wished I'd stayed home and practiced, even though I'd have lost a week's pay because staying home and practicing the viola doesn't count

as planned implementation of recreational lei-
sure as defined by the Federal Union of Unions.

When I came back from my Antarctican ex-
pedition, the man was reading again, and I got
a look at his pamphlet; and that was the odd
part of it. The pamphlet was called "Increasing
Efficiency in Public Accountant Training
Schools," and I could see from the one para-
graph I got a glance at that there was nothing
about new continents emerging from the ocean
depths in it—nothing at all.

Then we had to get out and walk on into
Gresham, because they had decided that the
best thing for us all to do was get onto the
Greater Portland Area Rapid Public Transit
Lines, since there had been so many break-
downs that the charter bus company didn't
have any more buses to send out to pick us up.
The walk was wet, and rather dull, except when
we passed the Cold Mountain Commune. They
had a wall around it to keep out unauthorized
persons, and a big neon sign out front saying
COLD MOUNTAIN COMMUNE and there were
some people in authentic jeans and ponchos by
the highway selling macrame belts and sand-
cast candles and soybean bread to the tourists.
In Gresham, I took the 4:40 GPARPTL Superjet
Flyer train to Burnside and East 230th, and
then walked to 217th and got the bus to the
Goldschmidt Overpass, and transferred to the
shuttlebus, but it had boiler trouble, so I didn't
reach the downtown transfer point until ten af-

ter eight, and the buses go on a once-an-hour schedule at 8:00, so I got a meatless hamburger at the Longhorn Inch-Thick Steak House Dinerette and caught the nine o'clock bus and got home about ten. When I let myself into the apartment I flipped the switch to turn on the lights, but there still weren't any. There had been a power outage in West Portland for three weeks. So I went feeling about for the candles in the dark, and it was a minute or so before I noticed that somebody was lying on my bed.

I panicked, and tried again to turn the lights on.

It was a man, lying there in a long thin heap. I thought a burglar had got in somehow while I was away and died. I opened the door so I could get out quick or at least my yells could be heard, and then I managed not to shake long enough to strike a match, and lighted a candle, and came a little closer to the bed.

The light disturbed him. He made a sort of snorting in his throat and turned his head. I saw it was a stranger, but I knew his eyebrows, then the breadth of his closed eyelids, then I saw my husband.

He woke up while I was standing there over him with the candle in my hand. He laughed and said still half-asleep, "Ah, Psyche! from the regions which are holy land."

Neither of us made much fuss. It was unexpected, but it did seem so natural for him to be there, after all, much more natural than for

him not to be there, and he was too tired to be very emotional. We lay there together in the dark, and he explained that they had released him from the Rehabilitation Camp early because he had injured his back in an accident in the gravel quarry, and they were afraid it might get worse. If he died there it wouldn't be good publicity abroad, since there have been some nasty rumors about deaths from illness in the Rehabilitation Camps and the Federal Medical Association Hospitals; and there are scientists abroad who have heard of Simon, since somebody published his proof of Goldbach's Hypothesis in Peking. So they let him out early, with eight dollars in his pocket, which is what he had in his pocket when they arrested him, which made it, of course, fair. He had walked and hitched home from Coeur D'Alene, Idaho, with a couple of days in jail in Walla Walla for being caught hitchhiking. He almost fell asleep telling me this, and when he had told me, he did fall asleep. He needed a change of clothes and a bath but I didn't want to wake him. Besides, I was tired, too. We lay side by side and his head was on my arm. I don't suppose that I have ever been so happy. No; was it happiness? Something wider and darker, more like knowledge, more like the night: joy.

It was dark for so long, so very long. We were all blind. And there was the cold, a vast, unmoving, heavy cold. We could not

move at all. We did not move. We did not speak. Our mouths were closed, pressed shut by the cold and by the weight. Our eyes were pressed shut. Our limbs were held still. Our minds were held still. For how long? There was no length of time; how long is death? And is one dead only after living, or before life as well? Certainly we thought, if we thought anything, that we were dead; but if we had ever been alive we had forgotten it.

There was a change. It must have been the pressure that changed first, although we did not know it. The eyelids are sensitive to touch. They must have been weary of being shut. When the pressure upon them weakened a little, they opened. But there was no way for us to know that. It was too cold for us to feel anything. There was nothing to be seen. There was black.

But then—"then," for the event created time, created before and after, near and far, now and then—"then" there was the light. One light. One small, strange light that passed slowly, at what distance we could not tell. A small, greenish white, slightly blurred point of radiance, passing.

Our eyes were certainly open, "then," for we saw it. We saw the moment. The moment is a point of light. Whether in darkness or in the field of all light, the moment

is small, and moves, but not quickly. And "then" it is gone.

It did not occur to us that there might be another moment. There was no reason to assume that there might be more than one. One was marvel enough; that in all the field of the dark, in the cold, heavy, dense, moveless, timeless, placeless, boundless black, there should have occurred, once, a small, slightly blurred, moving light! Time need be created only once, we thought.

But we were mistaken. The difference between one and more than one is all the difference in the world. Indeed, that difference is the world.

The light returned.

The same light, or another one? There was no telling.

But, "this time," we wondered about the light: Was it small and near to us, or large and far away? Again there was no telling; but there was something about the way it moved, a trace of hesitation, a tentative quality, that did not seem proper to anything large and remote. The stars, for instance. We began to remember the stars.

The stars had never hesitated.

Perhaps the noble certainty of their gait had been a mere effect of distance. Perhaps in fact they had hurtled wildly, enormous furnace-fragments of a primal bomb thrown through the cosmic dark; but time

and distance soften all agony. If the universe, as seems likely, began with an act of destruction, the stars we had used to see told no tales of it. They had been implacably serene.

The planets, however . . . We began to remember the planets. They had suffered certain changes both of appearance and of course. At certain times of the year Mars would reverse its direction and go backward through the stars. Venus had been brighter and less bright as she went through her phases of crescent, full, and wane. Mercury had shuddered like a skidding drop of rain on the sky flushed with daybreak. The light we now watched had that erratic, trembling quality. We saw it, unmistakably, change direction and go backward. It then grew smaller and fainter; blinked—an eclipse?—and slowly disappeared.

Slowly, but not slowly enough for a planet.

Then—the third "then"!—arrived the indubitable and positive Wonder of the World, the Magic Trick, watch now, watch, you will not believe your eyes, mama, mama, look what I can do—

Seven lights in a row, proceeding fairly rapidly, with a darting movement, from left to right. Proceeding less rapidly from right to left, two dimmer, greenish lights. Two-

lights halt, blink, reverse course, proceed hastily and in a wavering manner from left to right. Seven-lights increase speed, and catch up. Two-lights flash desperately, flicker, and are gone.

Seven-lights hang still for some while, then merge gradually into one streak, veering away, and little by little vanish into the immensity of the dark.

But in the dark now are growing other lights, many of them: lamps, dots, rows, scintillations—some near at hand, some far. Like the stars, yes, but not stars. It is not the great Existences we are seeing, but only the little lives.

In the morning Simon told me something about the Camp, but not until after he had had me check the apartment for bugs. I thought at first he had been given behavior mod and gone paranoid. We never had been infested. And I'd been living alone for a year and a half; surely they didn't want to hear me talking to myself? But he said, "They may have been expecting me to come here."

"But they let you go free!"

He just lay there and laughed at me. So I checked everywhere we could think of. I didn't find any bugs, but it did look as if somebody had gone through the bureau drawers while I was away in the Wilderness. Simon's papers were all at Max's, so that didn't matter. I made

tea on the Primus, and washed and shaved Simon with the extra hot water in the kettle—he had a thick beard and wanted to get rid of it because of the lice he had brought from Camp—and while we were doing that he told me about the Camp. In fact he told me very little, but not much was necessary.

He had lost about 20 pounds. As he only weighed 140 to start with, this left little to go on with. His knees and wrist bones stuck out like rocks under the skin. His feet were all swollen and chewed-looking from the Camp boots; he hadn't dared take the boots off, the last three days of walking, because he was afraid he wouldn't be able to get them back on. When he had to move or sit up so I could wash him, he shut his eyes.

"Am I really here?" he asked. "Am I here?"

"Yes," I said. "You are here. What I don't understand is how you got here."

"Oh, it wasn't bad so long as I kept moving. All you need is to know where you're going—to have someplace to go. You know, some of the people in Camp, if they'd let them go, they wouldn't have had that. They couldn't have gone anywhere. Keeping moving was the main thing. It's just that my back's all seized up, now."

When he had to get up to go to the bathroom he moved like a ninety-year-old. He couldn't stand straight, but was all bent out of shape, and shuffled. I helped him put on clean clothes. When he lay down on the bed again, a sound

of pain came out of him, like tearing thick paper. I went around the room putting things away. He asked me to come sit by him and said I was going to drown him if I went on crying. "You'll submerge the entire North American continent," he said. I can't remember what he said, but he made me laugh finally. It is hard to remember things Simon says, and hard not to laugh when he says them. This is not merely the partiality of affection: he makes everybody laugh. I doubt that he intends to. It is just that a mathematician's mind works differently from other people's. Then when they laugh, that pleases him.

It was strange, and it is strange, to be thinking about "him," the man I have known for ten years, the same man, while "he" lay there changed out of recognition, a different man. It is enough to make you understand why most languages have a word like "soul." There are various degrees of death, and time spares us none of them. Yet something endures, for which a word is needed.

I said what I had not been able to say for a year and a half: "I was afraid they'd brainwash you."

He said, "Behavior mod is expensive. Even just with drugs. They save it mostly for the VIPs. But I'm afraid they got a notion I might be important after all. I got questioned a lot the last couple of months. About my 'foreign contacts.'" He snorted. "The stuff that got pub-

lished abroad, I suppose. So I want to be careful and make sure it's just a Camp again next time, and not a Federal Hospital."

"Simon, were they . . . are they cruel, or just righteous?"

He did not answer for a while. He did not want to answer. He knew what I was asking. He knew what thread hangs hope, the sword, above our heads.

"Some of them . . ." he said at last, mumbling.

Some of them had been cruel. Some of them had enjoyed their work. You cannot blame everything on society.

"Prisoners, as well as guards," he said.

You cannot blame everything on the enemy.

"Some of them, Belle," he said with energy, touching my hand—"some of them, there were men like gold there—"

The thread is tough; you cannot cut it with one stroke.

"What have you been playing?" he asked.

"Forrest, Schubert."

"With the quartet?"

"Trio, now. Janet went to Oakland with a new lover."

"Ah, poor Max."

"It's just as well, really. She isn't a good pianist."

I make Simon laugh, too, though I don't intend to. We talked until it was past time for me to go to work. My shift since the Full Employ-

ment Act last year is ten to two. I am an inspector in a recycled paper bag factory. I have never rejected a bag yet; the electronic inspector catches all the defective ones first. It is a rather depressing job. But it's only four hours a day, and it takes more time than that to go through all the lines and physical and mental examinations, and fill out all the forms, and talk to all the welfare counselors and inspectors every week in order to qualify as Unemployed, and then line up every day for the ration stamps and the dole. Simon thought I ought to go to work as usual. I tried to, but I couldn't. He had felt very hot to the touch when I kissed him good-bye. I went instead and got a black-market doctor. A girl at the factory had recommended her, for an abortion, if I ever wanted one without going through the regulation two years of sex-depressant drugs the fedmeds make you take when they give you an abortion. She was a jeweler's assistant in a shop on Alder Street, and the girl said she was convenient because if you didn't have enough cash you could leave something in pawn at the jeweler's as payment. Nobody ever does have enough cash, and of course credit cards aren't worth much on the black market.

The doctor was willing to come at once, so we rode home on the bus together. She gathered very soon that Simon and I were married, and it was funny to see her look at us and smile like a cat. Some people love illegality for its

own sake. Men, more often than women. It's men who make laws, and enforce them, and break them, and think the whole performance is wonderful. Most women would rather just ignore them. You could see that this woman, like a man, actually enjoyed breaking them. That may have been what put her into an illegal business in the first place, a preference for the shady side. But there was more to it than that. No doubt she'd wanted to be a doctor, too; and the Federal Medical Association doesn't admit women into the medical schools. She probably got her training as some other doctor's private pupil, under the counter. Very much as Simon learned mathematics, since the universities don't teach much but Business Administration and Advertising and Media Skills any more. However she learned it, she seemed to know her stuff. She fixed up a kind of homemade traction device for Simon very handily and informed him that if he did much more walking for two months he'd be crippled the rest of his life, but if he behaved himself he'd just be more or less lame. It isn't the kind of thing you'd expect to be grateful for being told, but we both were. Leaving, she gave me a bottle of about two hundred plain white pills, unlabeled. "Aspirin," she said. "He'll be in a good deal of pain off and on for weeks."

I looked at the bottle. I had never seen aspirin before, only the Super-Buffered Pane-Gon and the Triple-Power N-L-G-Zic and the Extra-

Strength Apansprin with the miracle ingredient more doctors recommend, which the fedmeds always give you prescriptions for, to be filled at your FMA-approved private enterprise friendly drugstore at the low, low prices established by the Pure Food and Drug Administration in order to inspire competitive research.

"Aspirin," the doctor repeated. "The miracle ingredient more doctors recommend." She catgrinned again. I think she liked us because we were living in sin. That bottle of black-market aspirin was probably worth more than the old Navajo bracelet I pawned for her fee.

I went out again to register Simon as temporarily domiciled at my address and to apply for Temporary Unemployment Compensation ration stamps for him. They only give them to you for two weeks and you have to come every day; but to register him as Temporarily Disabled meant getting the signatures of two fedmeds, and I thought I'd rather put that off for a while. It took three hours to go through the lines and get the forms he would have to fill out, and to answer the crats' questions about why he wasn't there in person. They smelled something fishy. Of course it's hard for them to prove that two people are married and aren't just adultering if you move now and then and your friends help out by sometimes registering one of you as living at their address; but they had all the back files on both of us and it was obvious that we had been around each other

for a suspiciously long time. The State really does make things awfully hard for itself. It must have been simpler to enforce the laws back when marriage was legal and adultery was what got you into trouble. They only had to catch you once. But I'll bet people broke the law just as often then as they do now.

The lantern-creatures came close enough at last that we could see not only their light, but their bodies in the illumination of their light. They were not pretty. They were dark colored, most often a dark red, and they were all mouth. They ate one another whole. Light swallowed light all swallowed together in the vaster mouth of the darkness. They moved slowly, for nothing, however small and hungry, could move fast under that weight, in that cold. Their eyes, round with fear, were never closed. Their bodies were tiny and bony behind the gaping jaws. They wore queer, ugly decorations on their lips and skulls: fringes, serrated wattles, featherlike fronds, gauds, bangles, lures. Poor little sheep of the deep pastures! Poor ragged, hunch-jawed dwarfs squeezed to the bone by the weight of the darkness, chilled to the bone by the cold of the darkness, tiny monsters burning with bright hunger, who brought us back to life!

Occasionally, in the wan, sparse illumi-

nation of one of the lantern-creatures, we
caught a momentary glimpse of other,
large, unmoving shapes: the barest sugges-
tion, off in the distance, not of a wall, nothing so solid and certain as a wall, but of a
surface, an angle . . . Was it there?

Or something would glitter, faint, far off,
far down. There was no use trying to make
out what it might be. Probably it was only
a fleck of sediment, mud or mica, disturbed by a struggle between the lantern-
creatures, flickering like a bit of diamond
dust as it rose and settled slowly. In any
case, we could not move to go see what it
was. We had not even the cold, narrow
freedom of the lantern-creatures. We were
immobilized, borne down, still shadows
among the half-guessed shadow walls.
Were we there?

The lantern-creatures showed no awareness of us. They passed before us, among
us, perhaps even through us—it was impossible to be sure. They were not afraid,
or curious.

Once something a little larger than a
hand came crawling near, and for a moment we saw quite distinctly the clean angle where the foot of a wall rose from the
pavement, in the glow cast by the crawling
creature, which was covered with a foliage
of plumes, each plume dotted with many
tiny, bluish points of light. We saw the

pavement beneath the creature and the wall beside it, heartbreaking in its exact, clear linearity, its opposition to all that was fluid, random, vast, and void. We saw the creature's claws, slowly reaching out and retracting like small stiff fingers, touch the wall. Its plumage of light quivering, it dragged itself along and vanished behind the corner of the wall.

So we knew that the wall was there; and that it was an outer wall, a housefront, perhaps, or the side of one of the towers of the city.

We remembered the towers. We remembered the city. We had forgotten it. We had forgotten who we were; but we remembered the city, now.

When I got home, the FBI had already been there. The computer at the police precinct where I registered Simon's address must have flashed it right over to the computer at the FBI building. They had questioned Simon for about an hour, mostly about what he had been doing during the twelve days it took him to get from the Camp to Portland. I suppose they thought he had flown to Peking or something. Having a police record in Walla Walla for hitchhiking helped him establish his story. He told me that one of them had gone to the bathroom. Sure enough I found a bug stuck on the top of the bathroom door frame. I left it, as we figured

it's really better to leave it when you know you have one, than to take it off and then never be sure they haven't planted another one you don't know about. As Simon said, if we felt we had to say something unpatriotic we could always flush the toilet at the same time.

I have a battery radio—there are so many work stoppages because of power failures, and days the water has to be boiled, and so on, that you really have to have a radio to save wasting time and dying of typhoid—and he turned it on while I was making supper on the Primus. The six o'clock All-American Broadcasting Company news announcer announced that peace was at hand in Uruguay, the president's confidential aide having been seen to smile at a passing blonde as he left the 613th day of the secret negotiations in a villa outside Katmandu. The war in Liberia was going well; the enemy said they had shot down seventeen American planes but the Pentagon said we had shot down twenty-two enemy planes, and the capital city—I forget its name, but it hasn't been inhabitable for seven years anyway—was on the verge of being recaptured by the forces of freedom. The police action in Arizona was also successful. The Neo-Birch insurgents in Phoenix could not hold out much longer against the massed might of the American army and air force, since their underground supply of small tactical nukes from the Weathermen in Los Angeles had been cut off. Then there was

an advertisement for Fed-Cred cards, and a
commercial for the Supreme Court: "Take your
legal troubles to the Nine Wise Men!" Then
there was something about why tariffs had
gone up, and a report from the stock market,
which had just closed at over twenty thousand,
and a commercial for U.S. Government canned
water, with a catchy little tune: "Don't be sorry
when you drink/It's not as healthy as you think/
Don't you think you really ought to/Drink coo-
ool, puu-uure U.S.G. water?"—with three sopranos in close harmony on the last line. Then,
just as the battery began to give out and his
voice was dying away into a faraway tiny whisper, the announcer seemed to be saying something about a new continent emerging.

"What was that?"

"I didn't hear," Simon said, lying with his
eyes shut and his face pale and sweaty. I gave
him two aspirins before we ate. He ate little,
and fell asleep while I was washing the dishes
in the bathroom. I had been going to practice,
but a viola is fairly wakeful in a one-room
apartment. I read for a while instead. It was a
bestseller Janet had given me when she left.
She thought it was very good, but then she likes
Franz Liszt too. I don't read much since the
libraries were closed down, it's too hard to get
books; all you can buy is bestsellers. I don't
remember the title of this one, the cover just
said "Ninety Million Copies in Print!!!" It was
about small-town sex life in the last century,

the dear old 1970s when there weren't any problems and life was so simple and nostalgic. The author squeezed all the naughty thrills he could out of the fact that all the main characters were married. I looked at the end and saw that all the married couples shot each other after all their children became schizophrenic hookers, except for one brave pair that divorced and then leapt into bed together with a clear-eyed pair of government-employed lovers for eight pages of healthy group sex as a brighter future dawned. I went to bed then, too. Simon was hot, but sleeping quietly. His breathing was like the sound of soft waves far away, and I went out to the dark sea on the sound of them.

I used to go out to the dark sea, often, as a child, falling asleep. I had almost forgotten it with my waking mind. As a child all I had to do was stretch out and think, "the dark sea . . . the dark sea . . ." and soon enough I'd be there, in the great depths, rocking. But after I grew up it only happened rarely, as a great gift. To know the abyss of the darkness and not to fear it, to entrust oneself to it and whatever may arise from it—what greater gift?

We watched the tiny lights come and go around us, and doing so, we gained a sense of space and of direction—near and far, at least, and higher and lower. It was that sense of space that allowed us to become

aware of the currents. Space was no longer entirely still around us, suppressed by the enormous pressure of its own weight. Very dimly we were aware that the cold darkness moved, slowly, softly, pressing against us a little for a long time, then ceasing, in a vast oscillation. The empty darkness flowed slowly along our unmoving unseen bodies; along them, past them; perhaps through them; we could not tell.

Where did they come from, those dim, slow, vast tides? What pressure or attraction stirred the deeps to these slow drifting movements? We could not understand that; we could only feel their touch against us, but in straining our sense to guess their origin or end, we became aware of something else: something out there in the darkness of the great currents: sounds. We listened. We heard.

So our sense of space sharpened and localized to a sense of place. For sound is local, as sight is not. Sound is delimited by silence; and it does not rise out of the silence unless it is fairly close, both in space and in time. Though we stand where once the singer stood we cannot hear the voice singing; the years have carried it off on their tides, submerged it. Sound is a fragile thing, a tremor, as delicate as life itself. We may see the stars, but we cannot hear them. Even were the hollowness of outer space

an atmosphere, an ether that transmitted the waves of sound, we could not hear the stars; they are too far away. At most if we listened we might hear our own sun, all the mighty, roiling, exploding storm of its burning, as a whisper at the edge of hearing.

A sea wave laps one's feet: it is the shock wave of a volcanic eruption on the far side of the world. But one hears nothing.

A red light flickers on the horizon: it is the reflection in smoke of a city on the distant mainland, burning. But one hears nothing.

Only on the slopes of the volcano, in the suburbs of the city, does one begin to hear the deep thunder, and the high voices crying.

Thus, when we became aware that we were hearing, we were sure that the sounds we heard were fairly close to us. And yet we may have been quite wrong. For we were in a strange place, a deep place. Sound travels fast and far in the deep places, and the silence there is perfect, letting the least noise be heard for hundreds of miles.

And these were not small noises. The lights were tiny, but the sounds were vast: not loud, but very large. Often they were below the range of hearing, long slow vibrations rather than sounds. The first we

heard seemed to us to rise up through the
currents from beneath us: immense groans,
sighs felt along the bone, a rumbling, a
deep uneasy whispering.

Later, certain sounds came down to us
from above, or borne along the endless lev-
els of the darkness, and these were stranger
yet, for they were music. A huge, calling,
yearning music from far away in the darkness, calling not to us. Where are you? I
am here.

Not to us.

They were the voices of the great souls,
the great lives, the lonely ones, the voyag-
ers. Calling. Not often answered.

Where are you? Where have you gone?

But the bones, the keels and girders of
white bones on icy isles of the South, the
shores of bones did not reply.

Nor could we reply. But we listened, and
the tears rose in our eyes, salt, not so salt
as the oceans, the world-girdling deep be-
reaved currents, the abandoned roadways
of the great lives; not so salt, but warmer.

I am here. Where have you gone?

No answer.

Only the whispering thunder from below.

But we knew now, though we could not
answer, we knew because we heard, because we felt, because we wept, we knew

that we were; and we remembered other voices.

Max came the next night. I sat on the toilet lid to practice, with the bathroom door shut. The FBI men on the other end of the bug got a solid half hour of scales and doublestops, and then a quite good performance of the Hindemith unaccompanied viola sonata. The bathroom being very small and all hard surfaces, the noise I made was really tremendous. Not a good sound, far too much echo, but the sheer volume was contagious, and I played louder as I went on. The man up above knocked on his floor once; but if I have to listen to the weekly All-American Olympic Games at full blast every Sunday morning from his TV set, then he has to accept Paul Hindemith coming up out of his toilet now and then.

When I got tired I put a wad of cotton over the bug, and came out of the bathroom half-deaf. Simon and Max were on fire. Burning, unconsumed. Simon was scribbling formulae in traction, and Max was pumping his elbows up and down the way he does, like a boxer, and saying "The e - lec - tron emis - sion ..." through his nose, with his eyes narrowed, and his mind evidently going light-years per second faster than his tongue, because he kept beginning over and saying "The e - lec - tron emis - sion ..." and pumping his elbows.

Intellectuals at work are very strange to look

at. As strange as artists. I never could understand how an audience can sit there and *look*
at a fiddler rolling his eyes and biting his
tongue, or a horn player collecting spit, or a
pianist like a black cat strapped to an electrified bench, as if what they *saw* had anything to
do with the music.

I damped the fires with a quart of black-
market beer—the legal kind is better, but I
never have enough ration stamps for beer; I'm
not thirsty enough to go without eating—and
gradually Max and Simon cooled down. Max
would have stayed talking all night, but I drove
him out because Simon was looking tired.

I put a new battery in the radio and left it
playing in the bathroom, and blew out the candle and lay and talked with Simon; he was too
excited to sleep. He said that Max had solved
the problems that were bothering them before
Simon was sent to Camp, and had fitted Simon's equations to (as Simon put it) the bare
facts, which means they have achieved "direct
energy conversion." Ten or twelve people have
worked on it at different times since Simon
published the theoretical part of it when he was
twenty-two. The physicist Ann Jones had
pointed out right away that the simplest prac-
tical application of theory would be to build a
"sun tap," a device for collecting and storing
solar energy, only much cheaper and better
than the U.S.G. Sola-Heetas that some rich people have on their houses. And it would have

been simple only they kept hitting the same snag. Now Max has got around the snag.

I said that Simon published the theory, but that is inaccurate. Of course he's never been able to publish any of his papers, in print; he's not a federal employee and doesn't have a government clearance. But it did get circulated in what the scientists and poets call Sammy's-dot, that is, just handwritten or hectographed. It's an old joke that the FBI arrests everybody with purple fingers, because they have either been hectographing Sammy's-dots, or they have impetigo.

Anyhow, Simon was on top of the mountain that night. His true joy is in the pure math; but he had been working with Clara and Max and the others in this effort to materialize the theory for ten years, and a taste of material victory is a good thing, once in a lifetime.

I asked him to explain what the sun tap would mean to the masses, with me as a representative mass. He explained that it means we can tap solar energy for power, using a device that's easier to build than a jar battery. The efficiency and storage capacity are such that about ten minutes of sunlight will power an apartment complex like ours, heat and lights and elevators and all, for twenty-four hours; and no pollution, particulate, thermal, or radioactive. "There isn't any danger of using up the sun?" I asked. He took it soberly—it was a stupid question, but after all not so long ago

people thought there wasn't any danger of using up the earth—and said no, because we wouldn't be pulling out energy, as we did when we mined and lumbered and split atoms, but just using the energy that comes to us anyhow: as the plants, the trees and grass and rosebushes, always have done. "You could call it Flower Power," he said. He was high, high up on the mountain, ski-jumping in the sunlight.

"The State owns us," he said, "because the corporative State has a monopoly on power sources, and there's not enough power to go around. But now, anybody could build a generator on their roof that would furnish enough power to light a city."

I looked out the window at the dark city.

"We could completely decentralize industry and agriculture. Technology could serve life instead of serving capital. We could each run our own life. Power is power! ... The State is a machine. We could unplug the machine, now. Power corrupts; absolute power corrupts absolutely. But that's true only when there's a price on power. When groups can keep the power to themselves; when they can use physical power-to in order to exert spiritual power-over; when might makes right. But if power is free? If everybody is equally mighty? Then everybody's got to find a better way of showing that he's right ..."

"That's what Mr. Nobel thought when he invented dynamite," I said. "Peace on earth."

He slid down the sunlit slope a couple of thousand feet and stopped beside me in a spray of snow, smiling. "Skull at the banquet," he said, "finger writing on the wall. Be still! Look, don't you see the sun shining on the Pentagon, all the roofs are off, the sun shines at last into the corridors of power . . . And they shrivel up, they wither away. The green grass grows through the carpets of the Oval Room, the Hot Line is disconnected for nonpayment of the bill. The first thing we'll do is build an electrified fence outside the electrical fence around the White House. The inner one prevents unauthorized persons from getting in. The outer one will prevent authorized persons from getting out . . ."

Of course he was bitter. Not many people come out of prison sweet.

But it was cruel, to be shown this great hope, and to know that there was no hope for it. He did know that. He knew it right along. He knew that there was no mountain, that he was skiing on the wind.

The tiny lights of the lantern-creatures died out one by one, sank away. The distant lonely voices were silent. The cold, slow currents flowed, vacant, only shaken from time to time by a shifting in the abyss.

It was dark again, and no voice spoke. All dark, dumb, cold.

Then the sun rose.

It was not like the dawns we had begun to remember: the change, manifold and subtle, in the smell and touch of the air; the hush that, instead of sleeping, wakes, holds still, and waits; the appearance of objects, looking gray, vague, and new, as if just created—distant mountains against the eastern sky, one's own hands, the hoary grass full of dew and shadow, the fold in the edge of a curtain hanging by the window—and then, before one is quite sure that one is indeed seeing again, that the light has returned, that day is breaking, the first, abrupt, sweet stammer of a waking bird. And after that the chorus, voice by voice: This is my nest, this is my tree, this is my egg, this is my day, this is my life, here I am, here I am, hurray for me! I'm here!—No, it wasn't like that at all, this dawn. It was completely silent, and it was blue.

In the dawns that we had begun to remember, one did not become aware of the light itself, but of the separate objects touched by the light, the things, the world. They were there, visible again, as if visibility were their own property, not a gift from the rising sun.

In this dawn, there was nothing but the light itself. Indeed there was not even light, we would have said, but only color: blue.

There was no compass bearing to it. It

was not brighter in the east. There was no east or west. There was only up and down, below and above. Below was dark. The blue light came from above. Brightness fell. Beneath, where the shaking thunder had stilled, the brightness died away through violet into blindness.

We, arising, watched light fall.

In a way it was more like an ethereal snowfall than like a sunrise. The light seemed to be in discrete particles, infinitesimal flecks, slowly descending, faint, fainter than flecks of fine snow on a dark night, and tinier; but blue. A soft, penetrating blue tending to the violet, the color of the shadows in an iceberg, the color of a streak of sky between gray clouds on a winter afternoon before snow: faint in intensity but vivid in hue: the color of the remote, the color of the cold, the color farthest from the sun.

On Saturday night they held a scientific congress in our room. Clara and Max came, of course, and the engineer Phil Drum and three others who had worked on the sun tap. Phil Drum was very pleased with himself because he had actually built one of the things, a solar cell, and brought it along. I don't think it had occurred to either Max or Simon to build one. Once they knew it could be done they were satisfied and wanted to get on with something else.

But Phil unwrapped his baby with a lot of flourish, and people made remarks like, "Mr. Watson, will you come here a minute," and "Hey, Wilbur, you're off the ground!" and "I say, nasty mould you've got there, Alec, why don't you throw it out?" and "Ugh, ugh, burns, burns, wow, ow," the latter from Max, who does look a little pre-Mousterian. Phil explained that he had exposed the cell for one minute at four in the afternoon up in Washington Park during a light rain. The lights were back on on the West Side since Thursday, so we could test it without being conspicuous.

We turned off the lights, after Phil had wired the table-lamp cord to the cell. He turned on the lamp switch. The bulb came on, about twice as bright as before, at its full forty watts—city power of course was never full strength. We all looked at it. It was a dime-store table lamp with a metallized gold base and a white plasticloth shade.

"Brighter than a thousand suns," Simon murmured from the bed.

"Could it be," said Clara Edmonds, "that we physicists have known sin—and have come out the other side?"

"It really wouldn't be any good at all for making bombs with," Max said dreamily.

"Bombs," Phil Drum said with scorn. "Bombs are obsolete. Don't you realize that we could move a mountain with this kind of power? I mean pick up Mount Hood, move it,

and set it down. We could thaw Antarctica, we could freeze the Congo. We could sink a continent. Give me a fulcrum and I'll move the world. Well, Archimedes, you've got your fulcrum. The sun."

"Christ," Simon said, "the radio, Belle!"

The bathroom door was shut and I had put cotton over the bug but he was right; if they were going to go ahead at this rate there had better be some added static. And though I liked watching their faces in the clear light of the lamp—they all had good, interesting faces, well worn, like the handles of wooden tools or the rocks in a running stream—I did not much want to listen to them talk tonight. Not because I disagreed or disapproved or disbelieved anything they said. Only because it grieved me terribly, their talking. Because they couldn't rejoice aloud over a job done and a discovery made, but had to hide there and whisper about it. Because they couldn't go out into the sun.

I went into the bathroom with my viola and sat on the toilet lid and did a long set of sautillé exercises. Then I tried to work at the Forrest trio, but it was too assertive. I played the solo part from *Harold in Italy*, which is beautiful, but it wasn't quite the right mood either. They were still going strong in the other room. I began to improvise.

After a few minutes in E-minor the light over the shaving mirror began to flicker and dim;

then it died. Another outage. The table lamp in the other room did not go out, being connected with the sun, not with the twenty-three atomic fission plants that power the Greater Portland Area. Within two seconds somebody had switched it off, too, so that we shouldn't be the only window in the West Hills left alight; and I could hear them rooting for candles and rattling matches. I went on improvising in the dark. Without light, when you couldn't see all the hard shiny surfaces of things, the sound seemed softer and less muddled. I went on, and it began to shape up. All the laws of harmonics sang together when the bow came down. The strings of the viola were the cords of my own voice, tightened by sorrow, tuned to the pitch of joy. The melody created itself out of air and energy, it raised up the valleys, and the mountains and hills were made low, and the crooked straight, and the rough places plain. And the music went out to the dark sea and sang in the darkness, over the abyss.

When I came out they were all sitting there and none of them was talking. Max had been crying. I could see little candle flames in the tears around his eyes. Simon lay flat on the bed in the shadows, his eyes closed. Phil Drum sat hunched over, holding the solar cell in his hands.

I loosened the pegs, put the bow and the viola in the case, and cleared my throat. It was embarrassing. I finally said, "I'm sorry."

One of the women spoke: Rose Abramski, a private student of Simon's, a big shy woman who could hardly speak at all unless it was in mathematical symbols. "I saw it," she said. "I saw it. I saw the white towers, and the water streaming down their sides, and running back down to the sea. And the sunlight shining in the streets, after ten thousand years of darkness."

"I heard them," Simon said, very low, from the shadow. "I heard their voices."

"Oh, Christ! Stop it!" Max cried out, and got up and went blundering out into the unlit hall, without his coat. We heard him running down the stairs.

"Phil," said Simon, lying there, "could we raise up the white towers, with our lever and our fulcrum?"

After a long silence Phil Drum answered, "We have the power to do it."

"What else do we need?" Simon said. "What else do we need, besides power?"

Nobody answered him.

The blue changed. It became brighter, lighter, and at the same time thicker: impure. The ethereal luminosity of blue-violet turned to turquoise, intense and opaque. Still we could not have said that everything was now turquoise-colored, for there were still no things. There was nothing, except the color of turquoise.

The change continued. The opacity be-

came veined and thinned. The dense, solid
color began to appear translucent, trans-
parent. Then it seemed as if we were in the
heart of a sacred jade, or the brilliant crystal of a sapphire or an emerald.

As at the inner structure of a crystal,
there was no motion. But there was something, now, to see. It was as if we saw the
motionless, elegant inward structure of the
molecules of a precious stone. Planes and
angles appeared about us, shadowless and
clear in that even, glowing, blue-green light.

These were the walls and towers of the
city, the streets, the windows, the gates.

We knew them, but we did not recognize
them. We did not dare to recognize them.
It had been so long. And it was so strange.
We had used to dream, when we lived in
this city. We had lain down, nights, in the
rooms behind the windows, and slept, and
dreamed. We had all dreamed of the ocean,
of the deep sea. Were we not dreaming
now?

Sometimes the thunder and tremor deep
below us rolled again, but it was faint now,
far away; as far away as our memory of the
thunder and the tremor and the fire and
the towers falling, long ago. Neither the
sound nor the memory frightened us. We
knew them.

The sapphire light brightened overhead
to green, almost green-gold. We looked up.

The tops of the highest towers were hard to see, glowing in the radiance of light. The streets and doorways were darker, more clearly defined.

In one of those long, jewel-dark streets something was moving—something not composed of planes and angles, but of curves and arcs. We all turned to look at it, slowly, wondering as we did so at the slow ease of our own motion, our freedom. Sinuous, with a beautiful flowing, gathering, rolling movement, now rapid and now tentative, the thing drifted across the street from a blank garden wall to the recess of a door. There, in the dark blue shadow, it was hard to see for a while. We watched. A pale blue curve appeared at the top of the doorway. A second followed, and a third. The moving thing clung or hovered there, above the door, like a swaying knot of silvery cords or a boneless hand, one arched finger pointing carelessly to something above the lintel of the door, something like itself, but motionless—a carving. A carving in jade light. A carving in stone.

Delicately and easily the long curving tentacle followed the curves of the carved figure, the eight petal-limbs, the round eyes. Did it recognize its image?

The living one swung suddenly, gathered its curves in a loose knot, and darted away down the street, swift and sinuous. Behind

it a faint cloud of darker blue hung for a
minute and dispersed, revealing again the
carved figure above the door: the sea-
flower, the cuttlefish, quick, great-eyed,
graceful, evasive, the cherished sign, carved
on a thousand walls, worked into the de-
sign of cornices, pavements, handles, lids
of jewel boxes, canopies, tapestries, table-
tops, gateways.

Down another street, about the level of
the first-floor windows, came a flickering
drift of hundreds of motes of silver. With
a single motion all turned toward the cross
street, and glittered off into the dark blue
shadows.

There were shadows, now.

We looked up, up from the flight of silver
fish, up from the streets where the jade-
green currents flowed and the blue shadows
fell. We moved and looked up, yearning, to
the high towers of our city. They stood, the
fallen towers. They glowed in the ever-
brightening radiance, not blue or blue-
green, up there, but gold. Far above them
lay a vast, circular, trembling brightness:
the sun's light on the surface of the sea.

We are here. When we break through the
bright circle into life, the water will break
and stream white down the white sides of
the towers, and run down the steep streets
back into the sea. The water will glitter in

*dark hair, on the eyelids of dark eyes, and
dry to a thin white film of salt.*

We are here.

Whose voice? Who called to us?

He was with me for twelve days. On January 28th the crats came from the Bureau of Health, Education and Welfare and said that since he was receiving Unemployment Compensation while suffering from an untreated illness, the government must look after him and restore him to health, because health is the inalienable right of the citizens of a democracy. He refused to sign the consent forms, so the chief health officer signed them. He refused to get up, so two of the policemen pulled him off the bed. He started to try to fight them. The chief health officer pulled his gun and said that if he continued to struggle he would shoot him for resisting welfare, and arrest me for conspiracy to defraud the government. The man who was holding my arms behind my back said they could always arrest me for unreported pregnancy with intent to form a nuclear family. At that Simon stopped trying to get free. It was really all he was trying to do, not to fight them, just to get his arms free. He looked at me, and they took him out.

He is in the federal hospital in Salem. I have not been able to find out whether he is in the regular hospital or the mental wards.

It was on the radio again yesterday, about

the rising land masses in the South Atlantic and the Western Pacific. At Max's the other night I saw a TV special explaining about geophysical stresses and subsidence and faults. The U.S. Geodetic Service is doing a lot of advertising around town, the most common one is a big billboard that says IT'S NOT OUR FAULT! with a picture of a beaver pointing to a schematic map that shows how even if Oregon has a major earthquake and subsidence as California did last month, it will not affect Portland, or only the western suburbs perhaps. The news also said that they plan to halt the tidal waves in Florida by dropping nuclear bombs where Miami was. Then they will reattach Florida to the mainland with landfill. They are already advertising real estate for housing developments on the landfill. The president is staying at the Mile High White House in Aspen, Colorado. I don't think it will do him much good. Houseboats down on the Willamette are selling for $500,000. There are no trains or buses running south from Portland, because all the highways were badly damaged by the tremors and landslides last week, so I will have to see if I can get to Salem on foot. I still have the rucksack I bought for the Mount Hood Wilderness Week. I got some dry lima beans and raisins with my Federal Fair Share Super Value Green Stamp minimal ration book for February—it took the whole book—and Phil Drum made me a tiny camp stove powered with the solar cell.

I didn't want to take the Primus, it's too bulky, and I did want to be able to carry the viola. Max gave me a half pint of brandy. When the brandy is gone I expect I will stuff this notebook into the bottle and put the cap on tight and leave it on a hillside somewhere between here and Salem. I like to think of it being lifted up little by little by the water, and rocking, and going out to the dark sea.

Where are you?
We are here. Where have you gone?

THE TOR DOUBLES

Two complete short science fiction novels in one volume!